I0724939

AIR SERIES  BOOK 11

VOID

NOVELLA

AMANDA BOOLOODIAN

DEDICATION

Dedicated to two very helpful kittens.

CONTENTS

CHAPTER

ONE

Between worlds.

"Don't let go of my hand," Vincent demanded as he grabbed mine. "And don't stop for anything."

The dark atmosphere held an ominous weight. Vincent kept a death grip on me and dragged me, despite my stumbles in the loose dirt.

A creeping dread filled my heart, chilling it.

Bright sunlight had permeated our day, but when Vincent moved us between worlds we dropped into a murky abyss. Searching up, I found no sign of the sky, much less a sun that might light the desolation around us.

Through heavy gloom details came into focus as I rushed to keep pace. When Vincent raced around a tree, I was able to get a closer look. At first glance I thought the tree was bare, but I realized that impression had been incorrect.

It's possible that even calling it a tree was an overstatement. It was more like an over-sized stick with spiky bulges on the trunk. It towered up with no branches, and at the top it tilted and curled in on itself.

Vincent tugged my arm in response to me slowing down. "That one can't reach us." Vincent breathed heavily, but kept his voice a soft whisper. "It'll try, but that's good. Nothing else around here will attempt to attack until it's had its go."

Can't reach us?

"Is that--" I had no idea what to ask, which brought me up short. *Is the tree alive? Is it a plant? How can a tree attack?*

With Vincent's encouragement I increased my speed. My heart started to beat faster and the smell became more prevalent. It was as though rotted meat had been left lying around.

Maybe it had been--the haunting shroud of haze could be hiding anything.

"It looks like we're in one of the Bane Forests. Don't believe anything you see or hear. This is a hellish area and not a great one to jump into, especially with someone who shouldn't be here in the first place."

What he said came out as an accusation, which was an unexpected blow to my feelings, even through the building terror. There was nothing I could say, though, he was right. If I knew even the smallest thing about my surroundings, I'd be on better footing.

"Watch your step up here," Vincent said.

The warning was nice to have, but the terrain was littered with stones, and I stumbled anyway.

Vincent stopped and helped me keep on my feet. "Don't fall down and stay as quiet as you can."

He noticed my gun holstered and took the weapon without a word. An unaccustomed feel of vulnerability sunk hooks into me, which wasn't great in an environment I expected to erupt with hostility.

"Don't touch anything or talk to anyone but me," Vincent said. "When we do talk it needs to be quiet, fast, and infrequent."

"Is there something I should be doing?" I asked.

Vincent's gaze never landed on me--instead he unceasingly scanned our surroundings. "Anything and everything I tell you, at the moment I tell you to do it."

In our world, those words would have stoked a fiery anger inside me, but here, I felt both in the way and unwanted.

"Tell me what to expect," I said. "I at least need an idea of what I should be looking out for."

Vincent hesitated. "We're looking for a trail or path. Let me know if you see one." Vincent raised his knife and slammed it down hard next to me. The remains of an oddly shaped lump of brown had tendrils which were now curling much like a spiders legs do when killed. "And until we find that trail, we can't stop moving." Vincent grabbed my hand and once again we moved swiftly.

There was no way I'd be able to maintain a run for long. Not after the day we'd had.

Are still having.

"The others--"

"Don't," Vincent snapped. "While we're here, we're here. Your mind can't stray--at least not until we get to a safe haven."

Vincent and I had snapped at each other in the past—both of us were prone to bickering. However, he'd never snapped at me in a situation like this. Never when I was scared, worried, and feeling useless.

My spirit curled into a tight ball in a corner where hopefully Vincent wouldn't notice. Keeping an outward calm wasn't easy, and it became harder as my breath began to turn ragged. It didn't help that he was towing me along, causing us to move at awkward angles.

A loud thump shook the ground and I spun around to find

the source. It sounded as though trees fell, but the gloom hid everything.

"It couldn't reach us," Vincent said. "But this leaves us open. Be ready to run."

Run? I'm ready to collapse.

A bull-horn-like noise erupted so loud it shook the trees, ground, and us. My bones rattled and I pressed my free hand over one ear, trying to protect at least that.

When I tried to get my hand back to cover the other Vincent clamped down harder, not willing to let go. He might have said something, but it was wasted breath. There was no room for other sounds.

The cacophony died as though clipped with scissors, and the silence left behind was so deep I thought I might have gone deaf, which wouldn't have surprised me.

Vincent stopped short, caught my eye, and put a finger to his lips. He remained perfectly still, so I followed suit. The only sound we made was our strained breath. I trembled from head to toe, so remaining motionless wasn't possible. Still, I tried my best.

Around us a whisper of trees creaked as though blowing in the wind, but there wasn't so much as a breeze. A ruddy red light broke through the gloom, but I couldn't see a source. Some areas were lit better than others, but I didn't want to shift my gaze, worried I might inadvertently make a noise. Despite that concern, I couldn't help but tilt my head, seeing nothing besides darkness above us.

We stood unmoving for so long my back began to ache and my knees protested. A howl rose up behind us, followed by another crash.

I turned, ready to run, but Vincent's only move was to guardedly watch the landscape.

While he studied our surroundings, realization of where

we were sunk in. I looked everywhere, trying to spot danger. Having no idea what the murk obscured caused my brain to see menace in all directions.

The trees off to our left groaned louder. Vincent whirled around, and the jerking on my arm was the only warning I had to start running.

With my backpack on there was no way for me to see what we were running from, at least not without tripping and falling. I had no idea what happened behind us, but getting as far away as possible felt best for our health.

When we passed another spiky tree, the need to get away was amplified tenfold. A creature had been impaled on thorns the size of my arm. The decay made it too difficult to determine what the being might have been. Parts of the body were lost to decomposition, but the tree maintained a firm grip.

Either real or imagined, knowing the remains were there made the stench of the world a hundred times worse.

The rock-strewn dirt gave way to small growths. My chest burned as Vincent silently urged us on. The terrain slowly shifted again, becoming moss covered and spongy.

Vincent's breath became strained. Even if he *had* been willing to tell me more about the place, neither of us were able to speak.

Vincent pointed to something ahead, but one space in the twisted dead forest was the same as all the others to me. The murkiness began to thin, though, which meant I could see farther.

I wasn't sure better vision was a good thing. Out of the corner of my eye, I spotted something hanging high above, spiked to a tree. Instead of looking closer, I stared directly forward and tried not to make sense of the scene.

We burst out into the open and my feet automatically slowed, but Vincent didn't allow it. My muscles screamed as he wordlessly yanked on my arm. Brown grass crunched beneath our feet with each step as we ran through what might have been a field.

It didn't take long for me to see the destination Vincent had in mind. We pelted toward an enormous boulder, which I guess made sense. It might provide cover from whatever chased us, but it also made me uneasy. It was one rock, in the middle of nowhere—how did it get there?

I chided myself for letting my imagination run away with me and allowed myself to be pulled to safety behind the stone.

Panting, Vincent stripped off his bag and took mine, then dragged me down to sit. We both propped our backs against the stone.

He worked hard to catch his breath, but he didn't wait to check me over.

"Are you hurt?" Vincent's voice was cold and emotionless, which was unusual when we were alone.

"No." It was a one-word answer and he was lucky to get that.

He gave me one more scan before he turned around and discretely raised his head to see over the rock.

My chest burned. I rubbed it in a fruitless attempt to slow the beat of my heart.

"Come see," Vincent whispered.

I almost refused. Exhaustion, fear, and aggravation waved a flag telling me to sit still. Curiosity set the flag on fire and I turned around, leaned forward, and then tentatively poked my head over the rock.

The sight made my jaw drop. My mind tried to come up with something logical for what I saw, or at least something that lived in the realm of possibilities.

This was a thing of nightmares.

Vincent moved closer and put his arm around me while I tried to fully comprehend what he wanted me to see.

The dark forest had hundreds of trees which towered up out of the gloom. Most of them arched over at the top as though reaching for the ground. They had no branches and no leaves. Trees I could handle--even if they were weird ones.

Higher up, it looked as though someone had thrown a mountain into the forest. The rocky exterior soared above the trees. The surrounding bleakness clawed up the rocky side, making part of it difficult to see.

With a slight movement Vincent directed my attention to another huge mass rising above the forest floor. It was big enough to be a foothill to the mountain, but it appeared slimy and green.

The new mound also began to illuminate the area around it.

Trees similar to those in the forest were scattered across the hill. Thankfully I was too far away to see if they had the same sharp spikes, but they were curled in the same way, which told me they had to be similar to those we had passed.

Vincent pressed himself into me and held me tighter.

The trees on the slope moved. The whole slimy green hillside expanded, growing fat.

I couldn't turn away. Tendrilled trees rolled down tighter, proving they couldn't be plants. Once the trunks were wound tight, they appeared to tense--or maybe it just seemed that way to me. Seconds later the trees burst out, unrolling themselves with another earth-shattering uproar.

This time I put my hands over both ears, but I never looked away.

This is a creature, right? But why scream at a mountain? Why does the large mass hold the living hill's fascination?

A foreboding began to rise from my gut. My thoughts rolled

out, making the connection, though I didn't want to believe it. I tried to convince myself there could be two explanations. The first: there was someone or something alive on the mountain. It was huge after all. Whole packs of animals could call the place home.

Even though it held a kind of logic, I couldn't bring myself to believe this massive living hill aimed at something on the surface, though my second theory, that the mountain was somehow alive, was completely impossible.

The trees around the mountain shot up like javelins from the forest floor. Their curly ends became rigid with points so sharp that from my vantage point, they resembled weapons. High up on the mountain, massive, shining green orbs came into view.

I gasped and gripped Vincent.

Eyes! The mountain has eyes!

There were five shining beacons that blinked twice before going as dark as any Walker's eyes. The ground trembled and the enormous mass moved.

As we watched, the mountain's trees shot forward like javelins.

The green blob screeched as the weapons sliced through its side.

I turned, putting my back to the rock, and slid down, then covered my ears. The reverberation filled my body with dread and I was terrified it would never stop. The ground shivered. Another harsh tone added to the confusion. The roar lasted a few moments and then there was silence. The ground continued to tremble, but the bedlam was over.

Vincent remained perched where he was and watched without apparent concern. I wasn't sure I wanted to see anything else. Instead, I leaned back and studied the vicinity.

Giant monsters would have to wait. They were too big to process.

Darkness. I could start with that.

The environment where we hid was easier to contend with. The reddish glow was gone and the ground was dirt and, aside from where we sat, stone free.

Vincent sighed, but when I peered up, he had an air of excitement about him. As he slid down next to me, he said nothing.

"Is it okay to talk here?" I asked.

"I'm sorry I yelled," Vincent said. "We woke up the old man and there was no time to explain."

I had no idea how to start responding to the statement, so I ignored it. "Are we all right here?"

Vincent shook his head. "Nothing is safe until we find my sister and leave."

"It's going to be like that the whole way?" I asked, trying to keep the dread from my voice.

"No." He cupped my hand in both of his. "Think about it as having levels of risk. We'll go through an area and it might be a yellow zone. We'll keep watch, but we don't expect something to kill us on sight." He had a forced cheerfulness that was almost as creepy as the creatures behind us.

"Levels of terror is more apt."

One of his hands dropped away and he slumped forward. He turned somber. "The truth is, I don't know how we're going to do this, Cass. I'm trying to think of a way to make it easier, or at least less treacherous."

"Let's take this one step at a time," I said. "You can get us out of here alive, right? I mean, this is what you do."

"I'll do everything I can to get you through this world."

"Us. You're getting *us* home." I closed my eyes and laid my head back again. There was a next action, wasn't there? A one-step-at-a-time plan needs a next step.

I heard Vincent shift around, but I didn't pay much attention. The world felt heavy. I had used far too much power before even reaching this dark hellscape.

When did I last sleep?

"Cass." Vincent nudged me. "We can't stay here."

He stood, ready to go.

I yawned and used the rock as leverage to push myself off the ground. "I forgot what I was saying? Where are we going?"

"To find my sister. She'll know when I'm near and set things up for us to move back into our world." He focused on me once again. "We're going to avoid the cold areas. Go ahead and take off your coat."

I shrugged it off and handed it over, then pulled on my bag. A thought struck me and I stopped. A smile crept across my face.

Vincent raised an eyebrow and waited.

"I get to meet your sister," I said.

A tremor of a smile rose and fell. "Yes. You get to meet my sister."

Vincent adjusted my bag, but he did it quickly. When he pulled away, I grabbed him and tugged him into me. "You saved us."

He hugged me hard, then stepped back. "I traded one catastrophe to another."

"You're being a pessimist." Before he had a chance to reply, I switched subjects. "Which way do we go?"

"There's not much of a trail here. This marker is a crossroads of sorts. In this case we're taking the route that leads us away from Bane the fastest way."

Vincent took off, but at a much slower pace. It was even

more leisurely than our trek in the mountains after we found Boone.

The mountains—they already seemed distant. Despite Vincent's warning I couldn't help but wonder about our friends and family waiting for us back in our world.

Or, were they waiting? For all we knew they could be searching the rubble for our bodies.

Rider would know, though, right?

I stumbled, but stayed on my feet. Vincent was probably right; I should concentrate on where we were.

"So, your sister is this way?" I asked.

Vincent shook his head. "Directions don't work the same way here."

"But we're moving toward her, right? This doesn't seem like the kind of place where we should take the scenic route."

"We're closing the gap between us and her."

"Sounds close enough." After a few moments I felt the need to fill the silence. Talking was normal and this place wasn't. One glaring example of the peculiarity was next to me—I could swear a bush stretched out. "At least we have supplies."

"That's going to both help us and hurt us," Vincent said.

"Won't they help us survive?"

"We have them, and someone or something else will want them. I rearranged our things so our bags are less conspicuous."

"Don't the animals here get their own food?"

"The animals usually do. Sometimes they want that food to be you. The people are a little different."

"People? Like other Walkers?"

"Sometimes," Vincent said.

When he didn't elaborate, I started to say something, but he cut me off. "There's a ridge coming up that will give you a better perspective of this place."

Sure enough, our path slanted upward.

I sighed, not pushing the subject. "How long is it going to take to get to your sister's?"

For a while I didn't think he was going to answer. I yawned again and tried to ignore that I wanted to fall over and sleep right there.

"Time doesn't work the same way here," Vincent said after a while. "If I had been wearing a watch, it wouldn't work. Our radio and cell phones are useless. Each world has its own cadence. When we're closer to where those worlds connect to this place, or if we're near active portals time can become considerably warped."

"But there's--"

"We're between worlds. In this area alone there are hundreds of different dimensions."

"If you tried to take us back home right here, what would happen?"

"We'd end up in a different dimension. And probably dead."

That was more than a little unsettling. "Why not our world? I thought we weren't going straight back because we might get stuck in the middle of the ocean or mountain or something."

"Which is why we're going to my sister; to make sure we enter our world at the right place. But the ground we're standing on now isn't connected to our dimension. I can't tell anything about the closest world, even my sister can't do that, but I *do* know it's not where we belong."

Knowing we weren't connected to our world ratcheted up my anxiety and I kept looking behind us, wanting to see something that would remind me of home.

The dark shrubbery and vines weren't familiar. Occasionally there would be a tree with bare branches. I studied the first few, and they appeared to be real trees, but in this world, I was far from an expert.

"Don't we have regular cycles our body goes through? We eat when we're hungry, sleep when we get tired. Stuff like that. Most people go to bed then wake up and it's a new day." I yawned again. "Except when you're me. I'm not sure I'll make it through the day."

"Sorry, I didn't think about that. I should have found the caffeine pills for you when we stopped. We'll take a quick break up here."

It took me a few minutes to realize I still hadn't received an answer to my questions. Before I could ask again, the scenery in front of us captured my attention. The gloomy night came to an end up ahead and looked as though we would pass straight into fire.

"Vincent?" I called, letting my apprehension out. "Is this safe?"

He took my hand. "That's a relative term. Let's just say it's expected."

When we reached the peak light stuck me, and I stopped. In front of us, the world was bright for miles around and we stood high above everything. The landscape in front of us could have been some sort of junkyard. It was well lit, but there was so much stuff piled up that the ground was mostly in shadow.

The area next to it, however, was beautiful. Jewel-like tones flashed brilliantly. It was hard to take my eyes off it, yet I couldn't help but look behind us, where the land was indistinct from lack of light.

Vincent led me to a stone outcrop. He walked around it, poked the ground with his giant knife, and even prodded the stone itself.

"I'll get the caffeine. It may be best to keep it close at hand. Take in the view before the flare dies."

"Flare?" I asked as my eyes strayed back to the colorful region.

"There's no sun or moon here. There'd be no place for them to go."

"It's beautiful," I said. "Are there any safe places between the worlds?"

"It's not the type of setting you'd want to visit on vacation." Vincent sat down next to me. "See that ridge line over there?"

"Yes," I said, studying a curve in the ground that ran through the junkyard before dropping off and picking up again what had to be a mile or more away.

"That is a portal linking two dimensions," Vincent said.

"It has vegetation on it," I said.

"It's been there a really long time. That gap, that's where the connection broke."

"So, when Boone and I traveled to the gremlin world, when the portal was closed off, this is what it looked like over here?"

"Not exactly." The light started to dim and Vincent took my hand. "That type of portal is like the one we're sitting on."

I stood up and looked around, suddenly anxious.

"It's been inactive for hundreds, maybe thousands of years. But it's one long ridge, cut off on both ends. We have just enough light left. I want you to look up right over there."

Following his lead, I saw something very odd in the dying light. "It's..." Skies aren't made of land, but that's what I was seeing. "It's..."

A spot above us, darker than dark, caught my eye, but the parts that stretched out like the ground bothered me most. I began to feel dizzy. My stomach flip-flopped, and I had to jerk my gaze down to assure myself I was standing on something solid.

"The hill up there is a portal. Another old one."

I was still staring when the last of the light died.

Vincent hugged me from behind. "Don't be afraid."

"If there's no moon and no stars," I whispered, feeling the need to speak softly as shadows crept in, "how do you see?"

"We have flashlights if we need them."

"No. When you come here, you have nothing. Every time. You don't have flashlights or even a lighter."

"It's starting."

He took my hand and repositioned it to point toward a patch of what I had to think of as the sky. It twinkled.

"I thought there weren't any stars." More patches began to gleam, drawing my eye. Some were pale, while others glimmered as though rubies and emeralds were fastened above us. "It's beautiful."

And it makes it much easier to think that there's sky up there.

Something much like a cloud gathered around the glowing orbs. It was hard to determine if the illumination created it or attracted it, but the vapor also began to glow, filling the world above us with a dim gleam that merged together, creating a river of radiance.

The flow reminded me of the Path. I inhaled sharply, excited about the similarities, and wondered what we were looking at.

"Remember, I've got hold of you," Vincent said. It was hard not to notice his closeness when his breath landed on my neck. "Look down the slope below us."

There was no way it could be more beautiful than the sight above, still, I dropped my gaze.

It was the same. Vertigo hit. The ground stretched out in

front of me, and was mirrored directly above. Up above, a blue cloud blossomed around a small ball of light.

I felt dizzy and moved my eyes back down to the valley below, searching for anything that could distinguish it from the sky. Far to our left, something flickered in the space between sky and ground. Whatever it was, it began to stretch out its beautiful violet glow.

"This is amazing," I said, my heart beating faster than I expected. "But a little disorienting. Do people travel at night?"

"There's plenty of light, and it's not night. Just dark."

"But the sky and land are indistinguishable."

"It's been so long since I've brought someone new here that I forgot how much I enjoyed it." Vincent chuckled. "Experiencing it with you, I can honestly say I've never been happier or loved someone more."

I closed my eyes, blocking out the strangeness around me while Vincent turned my legs to jelly. He kept me in his arms when I turned and kissed him. We stayed like that for quite a while. Since Vincent said time wasn't the same here, it could have been a minute or a day. But it was perfect.

"It is truly beautiful. Why did you think I'd be afraid?"

"Some people tend to have issues when they remember that there's no sky."

I froze for a moment at the reminder, then stared around. When I turned straight up, I pulled Vincent tight against me.

Fire blossomed beside us. Instantly on guard, Vincent yanked my arm forcing me behind him and for once, I didn't object. The flames left me light blind, causing me to blink rapidly.

The air stirred in front of me and I instinctively backed up, bumping into Vincent. Sticky cords wrapped around me in the space of a heartbeat. I sucked in a tight breath, ready to scream, but never got the chance. My bindings cinched tight which dug into my skin and pushed out my oxygen. Within moments, my feet left the ground and I was ripped away from Vincent.

It registered that it wasn't rope slithering across my skin. Slimy vines wrapped around me as though a hundred years growth was condensed down to seconds.

A thick sludge was left behind wherever the creeping plant made contact.

Laughter bellowed up behind me. "It's our lucky day." The leer in the man's voice made me twist in effort to get away.

My night vision was returning, but I faced the wrong direction. I couldn't see Vincent, much less the stranger that found us. In front of me, though, was a person unlike anything I had ever seen outside of a movie. The vines holding me captive now made since—I was being held aloft by a living tree.

The person's branches were bare, but still looked beautiful...

Right up to the point the tree noticed that I could see again. The wood circling me clenched.

The moment I opened my mouth to yell at the horrible shrub, tendrils leapt inside, choking me. It tasted like wood coated in engine oil.

"Looks like you have some things I want," the man in front of Vincent said. His voice was gravelly and didn't sound human.

My chest burned and it was impossible to move as I hacked against the foul substance that had been shoved in my mouth.

Behind my captor, a blurry fog approached. Worried that it too was ready to attack, I thrashed around which was a pointless response, accomplishing nothing.

"Just take what you want and leave," Vincent said in a stony voice.

"Seems reasonable," the man said. "My leshen already has what we want."

Some of my bonds tightened, causing waves of heat and pain. When I tried to scream it was nearly soundless. The vile substance in my mouth along with the compression across my chest made it almost impossible to breathe.

If I used my powers here, between the worlds, there was no way I could know what would happen. With the life being squeezed out of me, though, it was worth the risk.

My vision started to go dark around the edges. Before I closed my eyes, I saw the hovering puff of light coming closer, appearing to reach for me.

"You know there's no way around this," the man said.

"You're right, there's not," Vincent said. His voice was void of emotion.

A few seconds later, the bonds around me loosened, and whatever had been put in my mouth was torn out.

I dropped hard to the ground.

CHAPTER

TWO

It felt as though my chest had seized up, but I managed a few reedy thin breaths before I started hacking.

Everything hurt. When the coughing stopped, I didn't move. My concentration fixated on the short, shallow breaths I dragged in while trying to ignore the rest of my body.

Then a warm light enveloped me. It was as though the Path had come to pay me a visit, wanting to say hello and meet me. For a moment I even thought I might be reading, but my powers remained closed.

There was a thud in the dark, outside my glowing circle. I couldn't muster enough thought to care what it was.

"Cass?" Vincent called.

I blinked and glanced around while trying not to raise my head. Finally, Vincent moved into my line of sight.

For a moment, he squatted down a few feet away from me and watched, as though he needed confirmation I was alive.

"Are they gone?" My voice came out scratchy and rough.

Vincent looked as though I kicked him. "They won't be bothering us again."

Tears welled up and ran down my face sideways. "Both of them?"

Vincent stared behind me. "You won't have to worry about either of them anymore."

My chest was on fire, but I closed my eyes while letting out a deep breath.

"I'm so sorry, Cass," Vincent said.

My eyes were so watery that I couldn't make out his face until he sat on the ground.

"When you're ready, please let me in. It's just to check for injuries. I promise, that if you don't want me close, I'll give you space."

"Of course, I—" I started to sit up, but groaned and settled back on the ground.

"Please, just a few minutes."

The shimmering cloud which encased me looked blurred and once again I was reminded of the Path.

Maybe Vincent was reminded of it as well.

I stretched my hand to him. After a moment's hesitation he leaned forward until he grabbed hold. His face remained stoic, but anguish rolled off him in waves.

"Let me look you over," Vincent said. "You've got to be exhausted. It's okay to stop reading the Path."

"I'm not using my power," I mumbled.

Vincent helped me roll over and I groaned.

"Anything feel broken?" he asked.

I shook my head. "I can't tell. I don't think so, but..."

"You've got to be burning through a lot of energy right now," Vincent said. He rubbed his hands gently over my legs, checking for injury. "I'll give you some space in a few minutes. Don't feel that you have to have to keep reading."

I resorted to shaking my head. Vincent backed away, and I

felt as though I was missing something. It was time to get up—well, sit up at least.

"You have a few cuts," Vincent said, grabbing the first-aid box.

I grimaced when fresh misery rolled over me in a sitting position. My skin made it feel as though red-hot wire wrapped against me.

When Vincent approached me, he stopped again. It felt as though he was unsure about getting any closer. My throat burned from choking and being strangled, so I waved him over to avoid talking. When he sat, he kept me at arm's length, only moving as near as he had to while he searched for any cuts.

"Who were they?" It sounded as though I had a pack-a-day habit, but when I tried to clear my throat it felt like I had swallowed glass.

"People I shouldn't have let get so close," Vincent said. "I know there's nothing I can say to make you feel safe right now, but we're going to need to move soon. If you keep reading, we may not get as far as we need."

I stared at him blankly. My mind had cocooned itself into a little ball and ignored as much as possible. Vincent wrapped a cut on my wrist and I couldn't help but think he looked lost.

Maybe I was as well and what I needed wasn't a bandage. I scooted over as best I could, then pulled him in the rest of the way to me. We held each other. It was me who shifted away, and the moment I did, Vincent moved back, worried.

"I didn't see what happened to you." Once again, I tried to clear my throat. "Are you hurt?"

He appeared to struggle with something. "No one touched me," he said at last.

I nodded and looked around. "Do we have any water? Is that something we'll have to worry about here?"

Vincent quickly grabbed his bag and pulled out a bottle.

"Water is sometimes hard to come by, but we'll be passing a place that has some. Drink what you need."

I nodded and drank, the water wasn't cold, but it was cool enough to soothe my throat.

"You were behind me," Vincent said. "I'm not exactly sure what happened, but are you able to stand?"

"Let's find out," I said, giving him a wan smile.

"Do you want to stop reading first?"

"I'm not reading."

Instead of giving me a hand, he took a step back as though sizing me up.

"I was going to try using my power, but I never got the chance." I rubbed my neck again. "Everything happened so fast."

"It's possible that reading the Path works differently between the worlds," Vincent said.

Talking wasn't an easy thing to do, so I just nodded and reached for him.

He hesitated.

I checked my skin, wondering how bad the marks were, but he took my hand before I got the chance to see much.

"We should get away from here in case these guys have friends," Vincent said.

The moment my bag brushed against my back I sharply sucked in air. When we stopped the next time, I was going to have to do a more thorough check for injuries. It could wait, though. I wanted out of this place.

We walked in silence, but I held on to Vincent. With my hand in his or his arm around me, I felt better, at least until I noticed how tense Vincent's body was. When I brushed his arm, he stepped away, not forcing me to let go of his hand, but leaving space between us.

I wasn't sure what was wrong with him. There were too

many possibilities to narrow things down without talking. He was obviously upset—with me, himself, the world, who knew? After a minute I let go of his hand. He didn't try to retake mine.

The ridge we had sat on grew smaller in the distance. What he had shown me, tried to share with me, had been beautiful. I felt a surge of anger toward the people who had ruined it. The glittering lights were still alluring, but they'd lost some of their magic.

It was sad that the special moment with Vincent had been wrecked.

A part of me had hoped we'd be going to the glimmering meadow. It was disappointing when Vincent led us straight through the endless miles of junkyard.

Clearing my throat still didn't help, but I had to try before talking. "Why is there so much stuff piled up around here?"

"There are a few places like this around. Portals break open sometimes. In some areas," he gestured to our surroundings, "it happens more often. Trash can fall through, especially if a hole forms."

"Hole?" I asked. The fewer words I used the better.

"No one knows exactly what they are, but there are stories about them. Most people seem to think they lead to an abyss. If we catch another flare, look up and you might get an idea of where it comes from."

"I saw large dark spots earlier." I massaged my neck, and decided that description would do.

"Those are holes. Where you get holes, you'll likely get broken portals and areas filled with junk like this one. We have to be careful around here. There are burrows everywhere."

Since I had a million questions, I wanted to ask more, starting with what lived in the burrows, but my throat ached fiercely. Sadly, I learned that if I didn't talk, neither did Vincent.

Towering piles of rubbish surrounded us and we were constantly forced to climb over or around items. Most of what surrounded us seemed old, but I had no idea what any of it was. There was metal, wood, glass, shaped rocks, and materials I couldn't put words to.

Walking through a huge trash heap with a silent partner wasn't fun. Add in constant flares of pain each time something brushed my raw skin, and the trek was truly miserable, leaving me wretched and cranky. It didn't help that time dragged on endlessly.

Even worse, I felt very, very alone. I knew nothing about this place, and I was an obvious burden and liability.

"I'm going to need to stop soon," I said, my voice coming out little better than a croak. My muscles started to ache fiercely, making my insides feel as battered as my skin.

"We should go a little farther," Vincent said. "From the ridge I saw water up ahead, but we'll need to prepare."

"Prepare?"

"We need to carefully check ourselves over. If even a drop of fresh blood lands on the soil, we may never get out."

Vincent climbed a small heap, and paused. He focused, not at me, but behind us. "Right down here," he said at last, going into a small hollow.

For the first time in what felt like forever, there was actual ground beneath my feet instead of various other materials.

I dropped my bag. "And it's safer here?"

"As long as we stay alert."

"Are there more people around?" I asked.

"There are no signs of them in the area, so we shouldn't expect anyone. If we pay attention, we'll have warning of anything approaching."

Figuring that was the best I was going to get, I pulled up my shirt to inspect the damage.

"Christ, Cass." Vincent discarded his bag and came over to me. Indentations pressed into my skin everywhere. He walked behind me and traced his fingers lightly across my back.

"Is it that bad?" I asked.

"It's not good," Vincent said. "Keep an eye out around us. We need to consolidate our supplies and get rid of anything we don't need."

"What should I be on the lookout for?" I asked, pulling my clothes back down.

"Anything that moves. Or anything that you sense might be capable of movement."

"Is everything here dangerous?" I asked.

Vincent thought that over. "The rocks aren't always dangerous."

"Really? What about the lights you showed me? Those were beautiful."

"They are," he said softly. "I'm sorry the experience was ruined."

"But before we were interrupted—when they twinkled and the clouds bloomed out of them—it was amazing. I've never seen anything like it."

Vincent didn't say anything. Instead, he took a shirt from his bag and started to tear it apart. Once he had the thing shredded, he joined me again.

"The further we travel from the junkyard the hotter it's going to get," he said. "*Really hot.* I think we should wrap the worst of your injuries and leave behind as much as we can."

Vincent had me lift my shirt again and he applied something gently across several areas of my back, before starting to wrap my midsection.

"What was it that grabbed me?" I asked.

"It's called a leshen. It wrapped roots around you. It looks a lot like a tree, and they're usually not something you want to run afoul of."

"I can see why." I couldn't help but rub my throat. Maybe it wouldn't have hurt so bad if I hadn't just gotten over being nearly choked to death by someone else back in our world. "What happened to it?"

Done with my midsection, Vincent started checking my arms more carefully. "You didn't see it after it dropped you?"

"No. I was too busy trying to breathe again."

Vincent flinched.

"Sorry," I said, instantly feeling guilty that I let my crankiness slip out.

He moved in front of me, ran his hand down my face, and gave me a chaste kiss.

The soft touch along with the way he stared at me was enough to ignite a small fire inside me—the good kind.

"I wish I could tell you things will get easier," Vincent said. "By the time we're done, I'm afraid you're going to see me in a whole different way." I wanted to argue, but he went on, "I'll double check your legs, but I think you're safe."

"What about you?" I asked.

"I'm okay."

"You never said what happened to the leshen."

"It was taken care of. Most of it disintegrated."

My mouth fell open. "What?"

Done with me, Vincent busied himself with his bag.

"How did it happen? Is it..." *How to I ask if it's something he'd done?* In the end, I tried something else. "Is that something we should expect?"

He handed me water, which I drank gratefully.

"There is a creature that living here which you may like," Vincent said. "There's actually a few things, but some are incredibly rare, and as far as I know, we aren't in the right place to spot one. Around here, there's a small species of animal that sometimes show themselves."

Knowing he was putting off answering my question, I decided to save it for later. "What are they?"

"I'm not sure if they have an actual name. My sister used to call them chox. This is going to sound strange, but they're like a cross between white foxes and chipmunks."

Those two images weren't merging well in my head. "How big are they?"

"Full grown they're a little larger than an average squirrel back home."

I couldn't tell if he was serious or not. "Are there a lot of them?"

"You'll usually only see one, or maybe two at a time, but when you do, you can assume there are loads more that you're not seeing."

"I'm having trouble picturing them."

Vincent gave me a half grin. "If we see one while it's dark, we might see it glow."

"Seriously?"

"I give you my word." Despite Vincent saying he had no injuries, he double checked himself.

"It's not all bad here, is it?" I asked.

Vincent didn't say anything right away. "There are... interesting things that try to survive among the rest."

"I'm looking forward to seeing a chox."

"They're supposed to bring luck," Vincent said. "If you see two or three, they may even lead you to food or just to a safer haven. I haven't seen it myself, but I've heard rumors. Maybe more rumors *of* rumors."

"Safe haven?"

"Hidden hollows in the ground or an unnoticed cave. Those sorts of things."

"Are those the types of places we'll stop at to sleep?"

Vincent picked up my bag and helped me into it before grabbing his.

When he didn't say anything I started to worry. "Vincent, where will we rest? How long will it be before we find your sister?"

"Getting through this area shouldn't take too much longer," Vincent said. "Whatever you do, though, stay close by."

He stood completely still for a few moments before quietly climbing up the last small slope we had been on. He focused behind us and something about his demeanor changed quickly. There was an intent and anxious energy around him, so I stayed as quiet as I could.

Without a word of explanation, he came back and started shoving things into a bag. "We should find water soon. From here on out, we'll take one backpack. Let's get out of here."

I stayed where I was while he started to climb the next rise.

"Why won't you answer me?" I asked, forcing him to either stop or leave me behind.

When he turned, he didn't catch my eye, and instead studied our surroundings. "It's a difficult question."

"Difficult to determine or difficult to tell me?"

"Both."

I raised an eyebrow and waited.

He ran his fingers through his hair and looked in the direction we had been traveling. "We've been here for over a day already. Barring anything unforeseen it'll take three more to reach my sister."

"And breaks? Resting, sleeping—what about them?" I asked.

"You don't understand the way things work here."

"Because you aren't telling me *anything*," I snapped.

Vincent took a deep breath, appearing to steady himself. "You're right. Let's keep moving, though. I'll try to answer your questions as we go."

"All of them?"

He sighed. "Any of them that I have an explanation for. But we have to start moving." He started to scramble up the trash pile again.

"Let's start with the basics," I said following him. "What are the first things I should know about this place?"

Vincent didn't reply right away, but when he reached the rise, he waited for me to catch up. As soon as we set out together, he began answering.

"There are three things to remember. First, if you find a trail, don't leave it unless you have to or unless it starts taking you too far in the wrong direction. The path might start to turn strange or scary, but don't leave it. Two. You will see everything in this world, many of which you didn't know could exist, but don't attack anything that's not attacking you. Even then be very careful. There really are some areas where a drop of blood hitting the ground will bring hellfire down on us."

"And three?" I asked when he didn't continue.

"Don't talk to the plants."

CHAPTER

THREE

My eyebrows snapped together. *Is he making fun of me?*

Vincent didn't crack a smile. "I'm serious. Do not talk to or listen to the trees, bushes, or anything. Some of them will do everything they can to mess with your head."

"Okay," I replied. "Stay on the trail, no letting blood fall on the ground, and don't talk to plants. Got it."

"If you see any animals or insects, let me know."

"Should I be worried about snakes or spiders?" I asked, suddenly leery.

"You don't have to worry about either of them—"

That was at least some relief.

"—they wouldn't survive long," Vincent finished.

I glared at the back of Vincent's head.

Vincent chuckled without turning around. "I told you I'd answer you."

As we trudged on, the air turned dense, and I started to drag my feet as my breathing grew heavier.

I was exhausted, but I needed more answers before I contemplated sleep again. "Will we run into more people?"

Vincent slowed and didn't say anything. When I reached him, he took my hand. His eyes were constantly scanning our surroundings. He paused and studied the trail behind us for a full minute before moving on again.

"That shouldn't have happened," he said after a while. He squeezed my hand. "I'm going to do what I can to make sure nothing else gets close."

I linked my arm in his and leaned against him. It wasn't easy with the backpack, and it didn't help our progress, but I wanted contact.

"Not all the people are like them," Vincent said. "But unless you know the person, don't trust them."

I loosened my grip on him and went back to walking hand in hand. "Do we avoid everyone?"

"Usually no, I don't avoid people. This place isn't exactly crowded, but you may run across someone who can give you information about what to expect. Sometimes people want to trade for something they need, or they just want someone to talk to. It can be lonely traveling here."

"So, we'll see more?"

"It's hard to say. Most people won't come near a Walker, and for now we want to do everything we can to avoid others. I can't take the risk. With you here, though, I think it'll be unavoidable. Your soul attracts anything living."

"Wait, so running into those two was my fault?" I squeaked.

He rubbed my hand, but his eyes ceaselessly roamed. "I didn't mean it like that. Those two were there for a reason, and it wouldn't have mattered *who* they ran into. They got what they deserved."

I sniffed, not wanting to think about it anymore. It only reminded me of how sore I was. Surprisingly, I wasn't as tired as I'd expected.

"What I meant was, people find you intriguing. Anything living will. They're drawn to you. So, even though you're with a Walker, we're likely to draw attention from someone or something."

"Do Walkers ever take anyone home? I mean, most of these people are stuck here, right?"

"Most of the people we'll run into were born here. I've never met anyone from our world that ended up here accidentally." Vincent squeezed my hand and stopped. "Don't trust people, but you don't have to assume they're going to hurt us."

The ground in front of us became clear of debris, only to be replaced by nothing. No junk, no grass, just gray dirt.

"Are there any towns or anything here?" I asked.

"There's one I know of, but I've never tried to find it. From what I've heard, it's a brutal place. Occasionally someone tries to build a different settlement, but it doesn't work."

The entire environment continued to change and the air became heavier and wet.

"Why's that?" I asked, glancing around us. Haze began to skirt around us making it feel as though we were being boxed in.

"This isn't a world. The rules are different here. There's no sun, and those aren't stars above us."

"Are they some sort of lights floating on the air?"

"That's what the flare is, or seems to be at least. The point is, we're between worlds. Portals are pushed through and can appear at any time. Once the pathway has been there for a few years, things start to grow on them and live there. However, portals can disappear just as quickly as they arrive."

The fog grew thicker the farther away from the trash dump, and on this spot, when I glanced up no twinkling lights shined.

"How do people get up there?" I asked.

"There are portals which push through the ground we're on and connect the areas. The portals have a gravity of their own. You'll get a better idea of what it's like during the next flare."

"What are the flares?"

"I've never known anyone who's certain. The best guess is some sort of creature. There's not a day and night—the brightness comes and goes randomly. There are quite a few things that create light in this world, but as you could see from where we started, they aren't everywhere."

I was having hard time imagining all this. I was hoping for a flare again to see if it helped.

Although, I guess it was a possibility it might only make things more horrible.

"Slow down," Vincent whispered. "I think there's something ahead."

I concentrated on our surroundings, but I had no idea what might be considered dangerous. There wasn't much I could see through the misty air, which didn't help. I did my best to check behind, making sure nothing snuck up on us while Vincent handled the front.

Every three steps or so I stumbled, though I watched as much as I was able.

Vincent stopped and I ran straight into him.

Since we weren't moving, I took my time to concentrate behind us.

"I think we're dealing with a few creatures," Vincent whispered. "Does the Path give you a better idea of numbers?"

Well, I had to try sometime. Usually, I closed my eyes to get to my source of power in order to reach out carefully. It wasn't necessary, though, and there was no way I would do that here. Instead, I watched for motion and mentally stretched to the edge of my knowledge of the world and—I glided straight into the Path. The transition was seamless. Even before my soul had been shattered, it had *never* been that easy to reach my power.

"How many?" Vincent asked again.

Tension rolled off him in waves, snapping me back to our predicament.

"There are two behind us, one beside and..." I swiveled around to see the other directions. "Three in front of you. I'm not sure what they are, but they're larger than a dog." One of the figures changed, growing taller. Although I couldn't see what they were, it was far too similar to what we'd fought back in the mountains of our world.

I shivered and backed up a step, which caused me once again to bump into Vincent's backpack.

"One of them stood up on two legs," I said, keeping my voice low. "What do we do?"

When Vincent didn't reply, I chanced a glance at him.

Reading a friend's Path was something I rarely did. I wasn't sure if it was the alien environment, the feeling of helplessness I'd been feeling since we arrived, or something I sensed from him, but at that moment I wanted to read Vincent.

It was a mistake to look. I shouldn't have done it. Vincent's Path showed a war within him.

A loud hacking noise came from the shadows, and the animals stalked closer.

"There's too many, I'm shielding us." Once I did I relaxed a little, despite my strength draining away. "I can hold this for a little while, but I can't say for sure how long. What should we do?"

"We have a few options," Vincent said.

I turned to face him, and since I had already read his Path, I didn't try to block it out.

The struggle inside him began to die away, but I wasn't happy with what was left behind.

One of the creatures pressed against my barrier, and I had my first good look at what we faced. The thing had leathery skin, but with tufts of hair sticking out like patchwork. It also appeared to have sustained burns at some point. The face was something straight out of a nightmare. Randomly spread across what could loosely be called a face were three mouths with razor-sharp teeth, and one large eye.

Another came near enough to make out features despite the gloom. This one had reptilian skin and only one mouth, but it had more arms than any one creature should.

"It looks like they were made in Frankenstein's lab," I said, not wanting to see any more.

"And they don't appear to be friendly," Vincent said. "That narrows down the number of things we can do."

"What's the best action to take here?"

"Disposing of them is the safest thing. It may be best to use the same method you did when our cabin was under siege."

I was so shocked I almost dropped our protections. Back in the mountains I had cut through a small army of monsters. It had been an act of butchery. Vincent said they never should have asked me to do it, but now he was telling me to repeat the atrocity.

When I looked at Vincent's Path, I could see a raw powder keg of power being tightly restrained. It was as though he was holding back.

"There's nothing you can do?" I asked, my fear doubling as other twisted fiends began to smash themselves against our shield. In the silence that followed the question, I started to shake. "You really want me to do this?"

"What I think is, you don't want to see me take care of them."

What the hell does that even mean?

My eyes burned when remembering the feel of killing all those monsters at once. I began wringing my hands. The creatures I had slaughtered before had once been people.

What if *these* monsters had once been people?

"Cassie?"

He never called me Cassie.

What is happening here?

I tried not to dwell on his use of my name. There were too many other things to focus on.

Closing my eyes didn't block my view of the Path, but it did take away my physical sight, which helped. No part of me wanted to see this.

Mentally I created a razor-sharp piece of air by turning it solid.

"I can—"

"Shut up," I said, cutting Vincent off.

I wasn't being fair and I knew it. If he killed them, they'd be just as dead.

But then, they didn't have to die, did they? We just needed them out of the way, giving us enough time to run.

Instead of a cage around us, why not one around them?

I turned, finding a direction to go, and I grabbed Vincent's shirt. "Come this way."

"You're burning through too much—"

These things need to be close together. Why didn't he see that?

"Then move," I snapped.

"Forget it," Vincent snapped back. "I shouldn't have suggested it. Stand closer to me."

It was difficult not to start yelling at him. I put that out of my mind, took a deep breath, and flipped over my shield, completely surrounding the animals.

That move drained me far more than I anticipated, but my aggravation with Vincent fueled the barrier.

When I tugged on Vincent's arm, he went with me. Finally, the animals came closer together, allowing me to use less of my energy.

Making the shield air-tight was harder than I expected, but it worked. As we moved away, the monsters lost their enthusiasm for chasing us.

They struck at the barrier, using up their oxygen fast. A few of the creatures fell to the ground, apparently unconscious. If I dropped the enclosure too early, all my effort would have been for nothing.

As a temporary measure, I quickly detached the shield from myself, but tied it to another Path. The work was more meticulous than I was used to, but after a few tries it worked.

The shield would consume the power of the attached Path, but it gave us time and at least they'd have a chance of survival.

"We can leave," I said.

"That was a good idea," Vincent replied.

"Let's go." I was just short of snapping at him again.

The fog obscured our vision, which was good for me. Vincent concentrated hard on everything around us, which should leave him little time to think about the jumbled mix of emotions which radiated from me.

He was hiding something. Vincent hadn't said he couldn't help save us. Instead, he thought I wouldn't want to see him take care of it.

And he was right. No part of me want to see the animals killed. *By either of us.*

He called me Cassie.

That was the root of my issue, I was sure of it. Before I went too far down the rabbit hole of worry and stress over a few words, I began to study our surroundings meticulously.

I didn't have to push away the Path so much as glide away from it. When I did, I noticed the haziness around us was lit and flowed much like the Path.

"There's water nearby," Vincent said.

After what felt like hours he finally spoke. As tired as I was, it was hard to care.

"We can refill our bottles." When I didn't say anything, he continued, "The steam is going to get worse, though. And hotter."

It seemed to bother him when I didn't say anything. My mind was full of questions, and I was worried if I started to ask them, I wouldn't stop.

The big thoughts tumbling around were the ones which involved Vincent. I had tried hard to put them aside, but the monotony of the fog let them creep back in.

From what I had seen of this world, there was no way he could have survived without being able to protect himself. So, why had he asked me to slaughter a bunch of animals? I didn't know if I wanted an answer to that one.

Again, I was still being unfair. Once those monsters began to attack, something had to be done. Why should I expect him to be the one to take care of it? Perhaps he needed to save his strength for rougher things to come, or maybe returning to our world was going to take all the energy he had.

I'm not sure I believed any of that, but I tried my best.

It was also a possibility that if I talked to him, he'd tell me exactly what I needed to hear.

The air grew thick with steam. My hair stuck to the back of my neck and my clothes clung to my skin, rubbing against my bruises uncomfortably. When I heard running water, I decided it was time to hold out an olive branch of sorts, even if it was only to break the silence.

"Why is the air so foggy here?"

"Magma. I haven't traveled this way in years, but there's a volcano nearby." His voice was carefully monotone and even.

"Magma? How close are we to it?" I asked quickly.

"Close."

"Shouldn't we go around?"

"If the area hasn't changed much, then this is the best route. On the other side of the volcano are the burning trees."

"Makes sense," I said, lightening my voice. "Volcanoes tend to catch things on fire."

"These burn all the time. With or without the volcano."

I had a hard time picturing it, so I said nothing.

Vincent stopped abruptly and turned, looking behind us. I couldn't help but turn as well, worried the beasts I trapped woke up much sooner than I imagined.

"What is it?" I asked.

Vincent shook his head. "Walk carefully. Between the water source and the volcano, it's possible for the ground to erode beneath the surface, leaving only a crust on top."

Despite what he said, he hurried on.

Heeding his words, I walked with a little more care, though we didn't have far to go.

As soon as we stopped, I sat down next to the running water, taking advantage of the chance to rest.

"I'll refill our bottles, but we're going to need to leave right away," Vincent said. "This could be the primary source of water for everything in the area."

I couldn't help but notice he dragged his feet while working, giving me a bit of extra time. I swallowed another caffeine pill, feeling as though I'd soon be running on fake energy and nothing else.

Once our water was replenished, Vincent went through the bag and repacked it. I'm pretty sure that was also a stalling tactic, but it didn't last long enough. Far too soon Vincent held out a hand and I reluctantly took it, and he pulled me to my feet.

He froze, still gripping my hand, and his whole demeanor changed. He appeared to be concentrating hard.

"Hello," Vincent said. He turned slowly and remained emotionless.

There was a clicking noise and then the sound of teeth clacking together. A person walked out of the hot, hazy air.

"I'm sorry," he said, for all the good it would do. "We don't speak the language."

Once again, I was glad Vincent put himself between me and the stranger that approached. The newcomer's skin was hard and the damp air made it shine. Feelers rose out of their bald head and pincers protruded from their mouth.

The insect person seemed rather nervous. Knowing the Path was simple to access here, I reached out to get a better feel for the situation.

It could have been because I had never seen the race, but their Path looked odd to me. It was definitely an intelligent being, not an animal, but there was something else mixed in there. It wasn't like Rider, whose Path was balanced between instinct and intelligence. The person in front of me felt even more primal.

I could also tell it took them a lot of effort to approach us. "He's scared. Well, he, she, whichever," I kept my voice quiet. "I don't think he would have approached us if he didn't need something."

"I don't think he's alone, either," Vincent said, not taking his eyes off the newcomer. "Get into my bag. We can spare a water bottle and some food."

The insect-like person scuttled back when I started to move around, but I grabbed what I thought we could spare. The bundle of supplies was awkward, so I grabbed one of my shirts and wrapped everything inside.

"Put it on the ground in front of me," Vincent said. "Then we'll move away."

I sat the package down and then picked up our bag.

The person clicked and chattered with renewed vigor and what I read in his Path made me want to open our bags again and dig around for more.

The insect person became less careful once we had given him space. Vincent tensed when he stepped forward quickly, still clicking his thanks.

"It's okay," I said. "He's relieved."

The person picked up the package and left something in its place. He drew back, chattering the whole time. He nodded a few times at what he had sat down and then waited.

Vincent carefully moved forward and took what was offered. The stranger chittered and made gestures. I'm pretty sure he was thanking us, but it was hard to say.

Then Vincent froze, as did the newcomer. The person's feelers twitched on its head, and both he and Vincent turned back the way we had come.

When Vincent unfroze, he turned and studied the rolling stream of water. "We need to find a way across."

The insect man said something and then backed away, getting lost in the haze almost immediately.

Vincent hurriedly moved along the water flow and I followed, but as it grew hotter, I lost sight of Vincent. If I held my hands out in front of me, they also disappeared.

Logically, I knew it didn't matter too much that I couldn't

physically see Vincent. I sensed him there, only a few feet away, but this world between worlds had too many unknowns for me to be comfortable having him out of sight for more than a few moments.

I tried not to let fear creep in and to concentrate on the feel of him and our bond together. It was bad enough I couldn't carry my own weight in this world. There was no way I was going to let myself become more burdensome than I already was.

A hand wrapped around my arm and I tensed.

"The water's too hot to cross here," Vincent said. "Can you get us over?"

I took a deep, shuddering breath, thankful he'd found me. "What do you mean?"

He slowed down his words as though I was slow on the uptake. "Can you use the Path to get us to the other side?"

I glared in his direction. It was possible he was getting as cranky as I was, but there was no need to talk to me as if I was a child.

My temper ignited. "I'm just surprised you'd ask. I know what you meant. You don't have to be a jerk about it."

"We'll need to go back the way we came," Vincent said, ignoring me. "Come on. We can find a way downstream."

"Will we be able to rest on the other side?" I asked.

"Not close to the river," Vincent said. "It'll be too difficult to keep you safe when visibility is limited."

I sighed. It made sense, but I didn't have to like it. "I'll get us across." *I'm not sure what condition I'll be in once we're on the other side.*

There was no way I was going to admit my exhaustion out loud. My power was the only thing that made me useful.

After a short meditation to calm my rapidly fraying nerves, I reached out to my power. Once again, it was laughably easy.

When I looked around, I could see the Path flow and dance around me, like an old friend. When I started to pull the shimmer tighter, to build something solid, it rushed to do what I wanted.

It wasn't only air which made up the bridge I created. The steam around us dissipated, as it too worked to build our passage across the water.

"Reading is different here," I mused.

This time it was me who pulled Vincent along. With the air clearer, I could see him again, but he paid little attention to me. His concentration remained behind us.

One thing that wasn't different about the Path was its effect on me. My strength leached away. Between my work earlier and this, I started to waver. My bridge held fast, however.

"Stop for a second," Vincent said.

"We're over the middle of a river," I said. It actually surprised me my temper didn't bubble up. "There's no stopping here unless you want us both to be cooked."

Thankfully, he didn't hold us back. When our feet touched the ground on the other side of the river, I let our bridge go. The flow dropped back into the Path where it normally would be, making the steam return right away.

I was so tired my bones ached. It was true I could read longer here, but sooner or later, there was always a price to pay. When I let go of the Path I stumbled.

"I've got you." Vincent dropped the monotone and he sounded more like himself again.

"Thanks," I said, leaning heavily on him. "I really need to take a break, though."

"As soon as we get away from the steam," Vincent assured me. "You've bought us some time."

"Is something following us?" I asked, looking back. It was a fruitless effort. Something could be a foot away and completely hidden.

"Nothing is going to be able to track us across a river."

"What's trying to track us?"

"It was probably one of those animals that attacked us. There may have been more around that we didn't see."

He didn't sound remotely convincing, but I was too tired to argue about it. Each step took more and more work than the previous.

"Is there a place where we'll rest soon?" I asked. "I'm not sure how much farther I can go."

Vincent looked around. "We'll try and find something. The air is clearing, but we need to get more distance between us and the river."

"Try?" I asked.

He stared around again. "Let's move on. There's not a trail here, but there's a portal ahead. We might be safe close to it."

It sounded like the best I was going to get, so I begrudgingly let Vincent keep leading me to wherever he intended.

After a while I decided to break our silence, if for no other reason than to stay awake. "Why would we be safer closer to a portal? We were on one earlier, yet it didn't seem to help."

"This is an active one," Vincent said. "It's currently connecting two worlds. If anything, living gets close to it, they're going to feel... uncomfortable. That means almost everything will steer clear."

"Where is it?" I asked, looking around.

"You won't be able to see it for a while."

"How do you know it's there?"

"I can sense them here," Vincent said. "It's one of the reasons Walkers survive between the worlds more often than people." Two more steps and he froze. "Don't move," Ignoring his own advice he turned, then his eyes widened. He shoved me to the side, knocking me off my feet.

I tried to soften my fall with my hands, but the rocky ground bit into them and I still ended up landing hard. Ripples of pain through my body from my earlier bruises and I couldn't help but groan. There was a chorus of mournful howls around us.

"Wait here," Vincent said.

Vincent walked away until he was enveloped with steamy air once again. It seemed as though I moved with exaggerated slowness while my body protested.

The atmosphere around me grew thicker—heavier—creating a threatening feeling that made me clambering to my feet. It became unnaturally quiet which had me scrambling to reach my power. Each direction I turned looked identical to the others. Trying to determine which way Vincent left was about as useful as catching fairy dust.

Scared, I reached out to bond with Vincent, wanting the reassurance of knowing he was nearby.

He wasn't. There was nothing. My chest seized. I pressed my hand tight against my heart, willing it not to break.

Before true panic could overtake all else, Vincent walked back into view. His eyes were slate black and he stared into the obscured surroundings.

But it didn't matter. I felt him there. Mentally, I cursed myself for letting my fear reach the point that I imagined our bond was somehow broken.

"I didn't get them all," Vincent said. His voice terser than I expected. "The others may not try again now that they know I'm a Walker, but we can't take the chance."

When Vincent strode past me, I saw the tear in his shirt. Blood discolored the fabric.

"You're hurt," I said, reaching for him.

"Shit." He looked down. "We can't stop to deal with it now though. They might come back."

I was too worn out to get mad, but Vincent's mood started to give me cause for concern. He walked off and didn't look back.

But I guess he didn't need to. The only choice I had was to follow.

I trailed behind for a while, but began to feel uneasy again and quickened my pace. When I caught up, Vincent's face was gray.

"Maybe we should rest here," I suggested.

"We don't stop," Vincent snapped.

I took his hand. "I really think you should sit for a while."

I only had hold of him long enough to feel his clammy skin before he yanked away. "You don't get it. I don't need to stop."

I tried to inspect his eyes, but he wouldn't look at me and apparently wasn't interested in anything I tried to say.

"I could use a break," I said, attempting a different tactic.

"Of course you could," Vincent said, his voice sounding snide. "Every god-forsaken creature in this hell wants to know what you are. Let's just sit here and let more of them come."

I bit my lip, willing myself not to be hurt by his stinging words. "You don't sound like yourself."

"Wait, you're right." Vincent turned on me. "Let's stop right here. Some monster will be by soon."

"We'll handle what comes."

"It's actually not a bad idea," Vincent said, almost to himself. "You'll attract anything nearby. Maybe if we use your fresh blood we can cast an even wider net."

"I'm not the one bleeding, and you're starting to scare me."

"Scare you?" Vincent's voice dropped and he took a step toward me. "You haven't even seen me yet."

His eyes were still jet black, which ratcheted up my worry.

He turned away and shook his head. "Let the monsters come. Or even the void. I can walk away, let it take care of you, and I can go home."

My eyes stung. "You're just tired."

"Tired? I don't get tired. I'm frustrated, stressed, and mad as hell. Do you have any idea how hard it is to keep someone like *you* alive?"

I winced. The words hit too close to home. "I'm sorry--"

"Of course you are." Vincent tossed our bag onto the ground, then swayed. "You always are."

I approached him. "You're not yourself. Sit down and--"

"Do you know what my life has been like since meeting you?"

"Well, I thought--"

"It's been hell. Straight up hell. Since I met you, people are around me and you're in my head, all the time."

My heart recoiled. He couldn't mean it...

But words like those had to come from somewhere, didn't they?

Mentally, I pulled back, trying not to listen, or to cut off the part of me that cared.

"Christ, I should have left you when I had the chance. Everyone would be better off."

I was being torn in two, but saying it wasn't going to help anyone. "Shut up and sit down."

"Although now I have to deal with a *new* hell." Vincent fell over. He hit the ground hard on his side and started to mutter. "Anybody would believe your death is an accident while we're over here. The elf will give me trouble, but Rider... He'd never forgive me. I can't win here."

I pushed him onto his back. He blinked up at me, his eyes flat black, but he wasn't seeing me. He only saw the horrors his brain tossed up. I put my hand on his head. It was no surprise he was burning up.

"Shit," I mumbled. I wiped the tears from my face and set to work. I gathered our supplies and pulled anything out that could be used for first-aid and piled it up beside me. I started to pull back his shirt, then stopped.

Were there contaminants in the ground? I couldn't take the risk, so I grabbed the sleeping bag and rolled him onto it. The steamy mist had drawn back, but the air was still warm. Vincent needed to be much cooler.

Like a mantra, I told myself over and over again that the fever made him say those awful things. I stripped off his shirt, hoping it would help make him cooler.

For the first time, I got a good look at his wound. An angry red gash radiated green lines under his skin.

Poison. Would poison put words in someone's mouth? Make them think differently?

His brain was being cooked. I grabbed something for the fever, an antibiotic, and water, then forced him to swallow the pills. Not that he put up much of a fight. When I set the water aside I thought about what to do next. A part of me was thankful he no longer spoke, but he had gone downhill so fast that it unnerved me.

Those pills needed time to work, and Vincent would need more than one dose. When I repacked the bag I made sure everything I might need right away—medicine, caffeine, water, and a weapon—was easy to reach.

There had to be somewhere safer than where we stopped.

When I touched his head again Vincent's hand snapped up and gripped my arm.

I sucked air through my teeth. "Vincent, that hurts." I tried to pry back his fingers, but struggled. He only stared straight up, his solid black eyes seeing nothing.

Though it seemed like much longer, it took only a few minutes for his grip to slacken, and then his hand fell away. I massaged my wrist and watched him fall asleep.

"I'm not sure what to do here," I admitted out loud. I spoke to Vincent, hoping he would miraculously tell me something useful. "If we wait here, will your sister eventually come? I don't even know how that works. She may not even have a clue that we're here." I stared at him while deciding what was next. "I guess we go find this portal you were moving toward."

When I stood up, I took in our surroundings again. Several yards away I spotted something glowing. I froze, my mind instantly imagining an awful beast ready to attack.

"You were right about a few things," I said under my breath to Vincent. "Keeping me safe is enough to wear anyone out."

The thing shifted and I put myself between it and Vincent. When it moved closer, though, I realized what it was and started to relax.

"You're a chox, aren't you?" My lips curled up, despite my predicament, but my eyes filled with tears. "You're adorable. Just like a tiny little fox."

It chittered, much like a chipmunk, then disappeared.

For some reason the absence made me feel even more alone.

The lights above twinkled, but as I watched, some of them disappeared. "It's getting darker," I said, talking to Vincent while he slept. "So far, the night hasn't worked well for me here. Does it get worse?" I checked the wound on Vincent's arm again, then wrapped it. "It's time to move. We're too exposed here." He made no movements. "We're going to the portal, if I can find it. If you have any other suggestions, I'd love to hear them."

Another sound made me turn my head. Six pale spots of light stood only a few feet away.

I sniffed. "You really are the cutest little things."

A howl rose up, and I turned around, though I couldn't find the source. The chox disappeared.

"I think we need to move," I whispered. "But carrying you isn't an option."

The only plan I could come up with was to drag him. I jumped up and adjusted Vincent so he was wrapped up inside the sleeping bag. When I went to grab our backpack, three chox were standing on it.

I glanced nervously in the direction I thought the howl came from. "You all may want to go, too. I don't think it's safe here."

When I carefully picked up our bag, they bounded off. Their presence worried me. No matter where I went I seemed to be a walking target. If they stuck around, they'd be in danger. Even in our own world, I wouldn't be sure I could save us, much less them. Between the worlds, I was going to get everyone killed.

When I turned back to Vincent, there were more choxes.

"I really think you'd like to see this," I said quietly to Vincent.

One of the choxes gripped the sleeping bag above Vincent's head with its teeth and whipped its head back and forth as though trying to tear a chunk out of it.

"You've got the right idea, little guy, but you should let me get that." When I leaned over, the backpack shifted painfully across my back.

A noise and the sounds of a scuffle came from nearby, but there was nothing in sight. I grabbed the top of the sleeping bag, dislodging a chox.

"Sorry." I sniffed, trying to make sure no more were in the way. When the ground cleared, I pulled, dragging Vincent. He was dead weight, but the sleeping bag made it easier than expected to slide him across the ground.

"I don't know where I'm going," I told Vincent. "Hopefully it's away from whatever sounds like it wants to attack."

Talking to him probably wasn't the best idea, since it only drew more attention to our direction, but I reasoned it didn't matter too much. Me pulling Vincent was far noisier than my voice.

Poor Vincent bounced across the ground, which became rougher.

I wasn't certain which direction Vincent had been leading us, but I was pretty sure I had chosen vaguely the right way. We had to move and keep moving, like Vincent said.

The choxes appeared and disappeared every few yards. They were company of a sort, and I didn't feel quite so alone when I saw them. It was also a reassurance to see something friendly in such a hostile environment.

Somewhere along the way I started following the tiny creatures. They led us into an area with stunted growths of trees and plants.

"I hope you're right about these guys being good luck," I said.

Vincent mumbled in his sleep. I was so surprised he spoke that my grip loosened for a moment and I fell over backward. The choxes weren't any more encouraging about my lack of movement than Vincent.

I rose unsteadily to my feet. How long had it been since I'd slept? How many bruises, aches, and cuts covered me? Numbly, I grabbed the sleeping bag and once again pulled.

All those things together didn't hurt as much as Vincent's words. There had never been anything certain about Vincent and me. From the day we'd first met it had been complicated and I was beginning to think I had tried to read way too much into our relationship.

Maybe what I thought was love actually came from me. Or maybe I imagined it because I wanted it to be true. Was it only our shared souls that kept him with me?

Chittering noises broke my revere. Looking in front of us, I discovered a wide expanse of water which brushed against a cliff. The choxes snapped at my heels and barked strangely at me.

"I can't take him through the water," I said, wondering why I had thought following animals was a good idea. "I'm not even sure it's safe." I let go of Vincent. "Everything is toxic here. I can't imagine the stream being any different."

Coaxed by the chox, which didn't seem hesitant about the water, I tentatively dipped my hand in. My skin didn't burn off or anything, which was promising. It was cold, but felt like normal water. What I needed was light enough to see what I might be getting us into.

Snarls came from the shadows near Vincent. Some of the choxes howled and jumped into the woods. Others ran across the water, proving that at least some portion of it wasn't deep.

At the cliff face they disappeared. I had no idea what I was doing, but I grabbed Vincent and pulled.

A growl rose up beside me. Without thinking, I tried to open the Path, but as exhausted as I was, I couldn't reach. My power stayed at a distance.

I dropped Vincent and peeled back the sleeping bag, going

for one of the knives in his boots. I pulled it out just in time to turn and slash an animal bowling into me.

Pain bloomed in my arm, but I ignored it. Fear and exhaustion stole center stage. I knew I had blood on me, but whether it was the creature's or mine, I wasn't sure.

The animal snarled again. I staggered to my feet and kept myself between it and Vincent. The creature was gray with dry looking skin. It was the size and shape of a large dog, but the thing's jaw set it apart from any animal I'd seen. It had a wide snout with so many teeth they didn't seem to fit in its mouth.

Dozens of choxes appeared and circled the creature. This time they didn't seem upset. In fact, they appeared to be having fun. The beast snapped at them, its jaw missing them by a hair's breadth each time.

Another little guy bit me on the ankle.

"Ouch," I complained. My clouded mind made me slow on the uptake. Soon, I figured out what the chox wanted. They were keeping the monster busy so we could get away.

Another howl sounded nearby, which spurred me on. Even if the water was poisonous, it had to be better than getting eaten by a monster.

That was, of course, unless they followed us. I could just be washing their meal for them.

The frigid water snapped my brain into gear. It wasn't deep, but with Vincent unconscious, it would likely only take a few inches for him to drown.

The cold sparked some life into him as well. He flailed, which wasn't helpful.

"Stop it," I snapped at him. It was much the way he spoke to me earlier, and my guilt was immediate. It worked, though. He stopped thrashing enough for me to get him across.

The dog-like creature on the other side of the creek howled its frustration and snapped again at the tiny animals around it.

The choxes we followed disappeared into a crevasse. After one last look at the fight across the water, I pressed on.

At first it looked so small I wasn't sure we would fit. I removed the backpack and placed it on Vincent, hoping it would stay until I could carry it again. Once it balanced on top of him, I slipped into the hole, dragging him with me.

I'd never thought of myself as claustrophobic, but that was before I crawled into a tight space, trusting an animal to lead me to safety. Half a dozen of those things could fit in one shoe box—what could they understand about space? By the time the entrance was out of sight I crawled on all fours, backwards, and was getting to the point where even that didn't work.

When my legs hit another water source, I panicked. There was no way to go back the way I came, since an unconscious Vincent filled that space.

My chest seized up. What had I gotten us into? I tried not to think about the fact that if this tiny tunnel ended at a dead end, there would be nothing I could do. Vincent and I would die in a dark, tiny hole.

I gasped when no air seemed to reach my lungs. A nip on my ankle made me realize I stopped moving. I had already given up hope.

But if there was room for a tiny little fox to goad me on, there might be somewhere I could go. Inch by inch I went through the water, scraping up my knees on the rocks and banging my head on the ceiling. When the darkness grew lighter, I actually cried in anticipation of an exit.

When I backed out and hit open air, I took a deep, shuddering breath and gave myself a few moments to calm my nerves. Finally, I took in my surroundings and saw we were in some sort of canyon. It was still dark, but I could see that there was actual grass. Even better, there were dozens of tiny choxes running around and playing. For the first time since going between worlds, I felt like my life wasn't in imminent danger.

Vincent began mumbling in his sleep, which reminded me he couldn't be counted as safe, and I needed him to get us both out of this horrible place.

I could almost picture me and Vincent back in our own world, maybe on vacation or just relaxing at home together. The idea needed to be squashed. What if he didn't feel the same way anymore?

Moving once again, I dragged Vincent through a short stretch of stream. Once on the other side, I grabbed the back-pack off him and dragged him farther up the bank. After that, my body wanted to collapse, but I had a lot to do before I could stop.

I unzipped the sleeping bag, opening it wide. The water we went through had been freezing cold, which seemed to have brought down Vincent's fever. Sadly, there was no way for me to dry him. I didn't dare take him off his nearly shredded bed, however. This place might feel safe, but if we needed to leave in a hurry, there were only two ways to move him: The Path, which would probably leave us both dead, and the sleeping bag.

I leaned over him and unwrapped his injured arm again. I sucked in air and whimpered, but caught myself and stopped. A chox came over and sniffed Vincent before yipping and running away.

The wound wasn't bleeding, but the skin around the bite had turned nearly black.

"That has to be the trick of the light, right?" I asked myself. "Or maybe because it's dark out?"

Using the ice-cold water from the stream, I cleaned the injury and Vincent's face.

By that point I was running on nothing but grit and determination. Any time Vincent made a noise it gave me a tiny jolt of hope--just enough for me to keep going.

"Cass, we need to go," Vincent said.

It was the first time in hours that he'd spoken in something other than a mumble. I felt his head and looked him over.

"Vincent," I said, trying to force my sleep-deprived mind to work. "You're sick. You've been poisoned or something. You've got to tell me if you know what this is."

"Cass... forget..."

I teared up and wiped the cool cloth over his face. "I'm right here, but you need to talk to me."

"Rider?"

He wasn't seeing me or hearing me. I curled up next to him and lost the modicum of self-control I had as I broke down.

Falling asleep had been inevitable. A person could only stay awake for so long and only do so much before there was nothing left but sleep. It wasn't restful, and I felt no better when Vincent woke me up.

The only word I heard was "Don't!" yelled from Vincent.

I shot up and searched around, but we were still alone. This time, very alone. I'm not sure if it was Vincent's yelling, or some other reason, but the choxes were gone.

Vincent was sitting up, but he stared at nothing.

"It's okay," I said. "Well, no, that's a lie. You should rest though."

"It's not going to be easy," Vincent said.

I sighed and felt emotionally drained.

He grabbed my arm. "I'll need help."

I tried to smile. "Always," I said. "Lay back for now. We'll get it taken care of."

"She won't like the assignment." Vincent's voice became more muddled. "She shouldn't know."

A part of me wanted to ask him questions, but my mind

was so fried I was barely coherent. Pushing Vincent gently back, I grabbed a rag and dipped it in the cold water before putting it on his forehead. Then I forced more medicine into him before he had a chance to fall back asleep. After that, I was at a loss.

"I'll ask her soon," Vincent mumbled.

"Should I be worried about this?" I asked, although I wasn't expecting an answer.

Knowing I couldn't go back to sleep without some sort of protection, I moved around, making sure to keep a close eye on Vincent. One of those bio-luminescent clouds hovered nearby. It was amazing how much it mirrored the Path.

Since the 'bio' part of bio-luminescent meant something living caused the glow, I didn't get too close—just in case.

It captured my attention, until my eyes started to cross and my surroundings became blurry. When I went back to Vincent, the cloud drifted closer, almost as though it followed me.

Vincent had moved his bad arm, so I put it in a position where he'd be less likely to hurt himself. I kept my eyes open, telling myself again and again I would stay awake.

Even though the idea of sleeping in this world made me cold with fear, avoiding sleep was a losing battle.

CHAPTER
FIVE

Something took my arm and I snapped up to a sitting position and tried to push away. My brain caught up and I realized it was Vincent. Looking around I took in the grassy hill and bright beautiful day which appeared so much like our world.

"It's okay," Vincent said, holding his hands up. "It's only me."

"Yeah," I said. "I think... I must have fallen asleep."

"I see that," he said, smiling.

I couldn't return the smile. Inside, I was torn up, and I needed a few minutes to get that under control. "How are you feeling? How's your arm?"

"Thanks to you, I still have one. And a body to go with it."

I shook my head and forced out a pitiful excuse for a grin.

"I thought I'd return the favor," Vincent said. "I didn't mean to frighten you."

I stared at him, confused, and he motioned to my arm. Somehow, I'd managed to forget being bitten by some sort of dog monster.

"Thank you," I said, letting him check the wound. "I should have noticed it earlier. I hadn't intended on falling asleep, though. It wasn't the smartest thing to do."

Vincent rolled back my sleeve. "There are times when it can't be helped. Do you know where we are?"

"In this world? I have no idea."

"I'm not sure I've seen a more secluded location." Vincent wiped away the grime around the injury. "Not between the worlds. I don't remember how we got here."

"That's not exactly surprising."

"I shouldn't have let those things get so close. I think they wanted to see you."

My nose curled up and I managed to harden myself a little more. "You mentioned that."

Vincent frowned and his forehead wrinkled up. "When I said other things might want to see you, this wasn't what I meant.

I glanced at him eyebrows raised, making sure he knew I didn't believe a word.

"I mean, I'm sure they were interested, but they would have attacked anyone. They aren't friendly."

I made a noncommittal noise and focused on the grass.

"What's wrong?"

My feelings threatened to slip out, but I refused to let them. "I'm not sure how long it's been, but you should take another antibiotic."

Vincent looked leery. "How did we get here?"

"I dragged you."

"Tell me what happened," Vincent said. He drew away from me, which was good. I needed the distance.

If he shut off his emotions, it would be easier for me to do the same. "You were sick. Really, really sick. After a while, you were mostly unconscious. You came to a little, but were mostly down for the count."

"What did I do?" His eyes seemed to narrow, but I couldn't look him in the eye, so I couldn't be certain.

Maybe I imagined reading his features.

"You had a high fever," I said. "You ranted a bit, and mumbled in your sleep. You weren't in your right mind."

He nodded, though it didn't look like he accepted it. "Did we travel far?"

"Honestly, I was so exhausted I'm not sure. I pulled you in the sleeping bag, but I couldn't say for how long." When he didn't say anything, I went on, "Is that going to be a problem? I'm fairly certain I took us off track."

He smiled slightly, and I turned away, no longer wanting to guess if it was real or imagined.

"You're not telling me everything," Vincent said. "Why not?"

"It's not important," I said.

"I'll remember eventually."

I nodded. "It can wait till then. For now, did I mess things up too much by taking us off course?"

"No, we're a little closer than we were, although I have no idea how we're getting out of here."

"Which is the only reason we're safe. If we can't get out, maybe nothing else can get in. I don't think much else knows about this place."

"How did you find it?"

I couldn't help but grin at the memory. "The choxes."

"You saw one?" Vincent asked, finally looking less troubled.

"They were adorable. There were *dozens* of them. They led me here."

"Dozens?"

I nodded and rolled up my pant leg. "They nipped my

ankles a few times to encourage me to go with them. When the monsters attacked, they're the only reason we survived."

"They fought?" Vincent asked, looking surprised.

"Well... it's more like they aggravated the creature. Distracting it long enough for us to cross a stream and eventually get here."

"This area is beautiful," Vincent said. "I've never seen anything quite like it between worlds."

"They ran around here and played, but I... I think they left before I fell asleep, though I don't really remember."

"I wish I could have seen them."

"Even when you were awake, you didn't really see anything. Sometimes I wasn't sure who you were talking to."

"I didn't..." Vincent shifted and turned away, putting away the few supplies he had been using. "I didn't hurt anyone, did I?"

"You didn't."

He cleared his throat. "I'm not sure what I said, or did, but maybe you should let me know."

"It's not important," I said, then yawned. "And I'm still exhausted. Is there any chance this place is safe enough to stay awhile?"

"I'll keep guard. If I see anything that makes me think we should move on, I'll wake you up."

"You've been sick, though. I think you need rest."

"Don't worry about me."

"I'm not sure I'll ever be able to stop," I said truthfully.

There was a hint of an embarrassed smile before he turned away. "Get some sleep. Rider and Logan are going to be worried if we take too long getting back."

"I didn't think about that. Maybe we should go on."

Vincent shook his head. "This might be our last chance to

stop and rest. We'll take advantage of it, and that will make it easier to finish the trip."

"Doesn't that mean rest for you, too?

He shook his head. "I don't really need rest here. Unless I'm injured like I was earlier, I never sleep between the worlds."

"Is that because you're a Walker?"

At first, I didn't think he'd answer.

"It is," he said at last.

Sensing his discomfort, I changed gears. "Still, take it easy until you're better."

IT COULDN'T LAST FOREVER. I knew that, but I didn't want to leave. Not only was the atmosphere horrible outside the little oasis, but during our respite, I could sleep, which I took advantage of.

Vincent found a way out of the small canyon through a crevasse almost hidden from view. He didn't trust the cave we used to enter the canyon, though I wasn't sure if he thought someone would ambush us or if it took us in the wrong direction.

He didn't scout far. He said he didn't want to lose sight of me, which was kind of sweet, but also a little reminder of how bad off I'd be if he left me behind. I smiled and said nothing, but it made it easier to push away some of my feelings for Vincent, good or bad, at least for the time being.

While exiting, we had to walk sideways through some of the gap and even had to climb over a few boulders. It was dim, but not dark, thanks to the flare lighting the world. Still, the deeper we went the more tense Vincent became.

And of course, the more uneasy Vincent grew, the more I worried.

"Will you be able to find this place again if you travel between the worlds in this area?" I asked, trying to focus on something easy.

"It's possible, but not likely," Vincent said. "The land here doesn't always stay still."

"It shifts around?"

Vincent didn't respond right away. We had reached the end of the passage and he stopped short.

I could see why. Over his shoulder I spotted a field of enormous flowers. It was covered in tulips, lilies, and sunflowers--except flowers don't grow to be the size of houses.

Yellows, reds, and oranges made up the flowered forest.

When I breathed in, the floral scent filled me. "It's beautiful."

"It is," Vincent agreed. "It's also tricky to navigate and... well, it's a strange place in general."

"You've been here before?"

"Look that way." Vincent pointed down the rolling hill. "See where the mushrooms start?"

They were enormous red-topped mushrooms with large white spots which easily rose as tall as the flowers. It was like watching something from a book come to life.

"I haven't been this deep into the flower fields, but the mushrooms should eventually lead into a forest. I wish we could avoid that place altogether, but that's the way we need to go. We'll at least try to circle around to avoid the deepest part of the woods."

"What should I be on the lookout for here?" I asked.

Vincent took my hand and led me under the petal canopy. "One of the obvious things to notice is the smell. This area is okay, but if you start smelling anything really good, or really bad, avoid it."

"Do those smells mean they're poisonous?"

"No. Here it means the plant is trying to lure in food with a good smell—or, if it's a bad smell, they already have something that's decaying."

My nose crinkled up and I looked more closely at the flower beside us. "They're carnivorous?"

"Only some of them."

"Got it. Avoid the smells."

"Aside from that, if you talk to *anything*, be sure not to automatically believe what they say."

"What do you mean by *anything*?"

"It's possible to run into things that aren't people, but they really can't be called animals or plants either. There are also animals that can mimic people."

"I'm not sure I understand," I admitted.

"Hopefully, we won't run into anyone or anything."

We walked silently through the brightly lit field for a few miles. Every now and again I'd try to see the flare in an attempt to get an idea of what actually caused the light. The floral canopy made it hard to see anything, which was probably a good thing. I tripped over my feet almost any time I looked around.

There were also two large circles in the sky. Vincent told me he thought they were portals which had somehow broken off, but were still open. He hadn't seen one up close. From the ground it looked as though the holes fell into nothingness.

The flower field wasn't as peaceful as the oasis we had left, but it was better than any other place I'd seen up to that point. Surrounded by such amazing plants, I felt comfortable and at an odd sort of peace.

"We should talk about earlier," Vincent said.

"By the tone of your voice I'm guessing you don't mean the canyon we just left," I said, trying not to lose the lighter feeling I had.

"Before that."

When he didn't continue I jumped in, attempting to put him more at ease. "Don't worry about what you said. You weren't yourself."

Vincent stopped and stared at me. "What did I say?"

He sounded confused, which I hadn't expected. "I think we're talking about two different things. What was it that you wanted to talk about?"

"I shouldn't have left you by yourself," Vincent said, still not moving. "Before I got hurt, we needed to stay together, but I walked away. I shouldn't have done that."

In an effort to keep him going, I kept walking. "This place is really strange. You did what you thought was right at the time." We needed a change in topic. "Are we looking for a trail again?"

I slowed down to let him take the lead. He did, but moved at a much slower pace.

"If we find one, we'll take it, but we aren't in too much danger here. Actually, no. That's not true. It's less likely that something is going to attack us without warning."

"Then what makes it bad?"

"Part of it is the scale," Vincent said. "Large flowers and mushrooms can mean large bugs or animals calling this place home."

"Like the person we met..." I was going to say yesterday, or the other day, but it was hard to tell how long we'd been in this world. "The person we helped by the river," I finished lamely.

"He seemed fairly new to this place, so I don't think so. It's possible though."

"Does everyone constantly roam around? Does anyone have an actual home in this world?"

"People try, but a lot of time it's safer to keep moving."

"If they stayed still, they could set up defenses."

"Defenses against animals and people is a good reason to remain in one place," Vincent said. "But it's also makes you easier to find. People who live between the worlds tend to be violent. They take what they want from anyone or anything weaker than themselves."

"That's awful."

"This life is all some of them have ever known. There are no rules here, and no laws. The first people we ran into when we arrived were truly a mild representation of what you can find here."

I shivered and moved closer to him. He took my hand, which I appreciated, but it wasn't helping me distance myself from him. If I let myself get too close again I might never come back from it. A part of me wanted that--most of me, in fact-- but when he left later it would hurt even worse. I let go of him quicker than I intended.

Vincent slowed. "I didn't mean to scare you. Only explain."

"It's okay," I said, trying to keep my voice level.

Vincent looked uncertain, but kept going. "It's not only the people you need to worry about between the worlds. Here, the environment warps and moves. When a portal comes through, whole areas can be destroyed or taken over by something else."

"But can't they bore through anywhere? Wouldn't they be a danger if you moved around as well?" I asked.

"It is, but if you survive, you don't lose as much."

"Because there's nothing to lose."

"In places like this, though, there's a lot more animals," Vincent said, shifting the subject back to our surroundings. "They tend to congregate to have a better chance of survival and plants mean water."

Vincent grabbed my hand, pulling me to a stop. He stared behind us.

"What's wrong?" I asked.

Vincent watched a few moments longer. "Nothing." He dropped my hand, looking troubled, and moved on.

It was impossible not to notice he moved at a faster pace.

"Is there something following us?" I asked.

"In this world, always assume something is tracking you, or waiting to ambush you."

"That's not an answer."

"It's the best I can give you," he said.

"You mean it's the best you're *going* to give me."

"Something like that."

I felt his aggravation rise, and I cut off the connection, building walls around it until nothing came through.

"Sorry, I shouldn't have said that." Vincent rubbed his chest and slowed down.

"It doesn't matter," I said.

He gave me a curious look. "It does." I only shrugged, and when I didn't say anything he stopped. "What are you doing?"

My head started to ache, but so was the rest of my body. The stop was welcome. "I'm following you. What else am I supposed to be doing?"

"Listen, Cass," he said, reaching out and taking my hand. "We're going to get out of here." He cupped my hand in both of his and rubbed the back of it. Then he stared at them frowning. "This doesn't feel right."

He wasn't wrong. For once, our energy didn't meld. There was no tingling sensation and no warmth spreading. He reached out and took my other hand, then gripped them hard.

I gasped at the unexpected pain.

"You're not her," Vincent said.

"Of course I'm me." When I glared at him I saw his eyes were flat black, but there was also another change. Black lines began to crawl across his face, going up into the hairline and down the neck, disappearing under his clothes.

He yanked me forward to stare in my eyes, while grinding the bones of my hand.

"That hurts," I warned. "Let me go now."

He stared into my eyes and his grip loosened. The black drained away.

"I don't understand," he said.

My bones felt like they'd been shoved through a grinder, and they hurt even worse when I moved them. Ignoring the pain, I yanked my hands out of his then pushed him away.

He let himself step back, but I put even more distance between us.

"What the hell?" I snapped.

"You didn't notice a difference?" he asked, his voice strained. "Something's wrong."

"So, you try to break my hands?" I yelled.

He stared at me, and soon the worry drained away from his expression. "Unless you did this on purpose."

I glared at him and said nothing.

"I see," he said. He watched me a moment longer, then took off his bag and found a painkiller. He shook the bottle then held out a few pills. "Take these," he said, his voice emotionless. "I'm not going to touch you."

"I'm not worried about you touching me," I snapped, grabbing the pills. "I'm pissed off."

He said nothing, but handed over the water bottle. I drank and shoved it back in his direction. Mutely, he took it back and put it away before shouldering the bag again.

"Ready?" he asked.

"Does it matter?"

Once again, he said nothing and only waited for a response.

I rolled my eyes and shook my head. "Fine. I'm ready."

He turned and walked away.

CHAPTER

SIX

It didn't matter that I couldn't sense Vincent. I knew him well enough to know I had hurt him.

And I felt *guilty* about it. How is that fair?

Twice I opened my mouth to apologize, but closed it again in a frustrated huff, which made me want to yell at him, or explain, or something. Instead, we walked in silence for what seemed like hours.

To keep myself from talking, I tried to meditate while on the move. It mostly made me trip over my own feet, so I gave up.

When I started to get tired, I almost asked how much farther we had, but bit back the words.

Vincent stopped and lifted a hand, signaling me to do the same. For a while I didn't notice anything. Then the ground shook and a noise like trees falling over reached us.

"Stay here," Vincent said. He dropped the bag and ran to a flower. In our world there would have been fine hairs along its stem. Here, he climbed them as though they were as sturdy as tree branches.

When he reached the top, I realized he'd chosen the tallest flower and could see over the others.

Apparently, he didn't like what he saw, and he rushed down the plant. About midway Vincent's feet slid off their limb. I sucked in a breath and held it, watching him fall a few feet before crashing into another thick obscenely large strand on the flower's stem.

He bounced and before he slid off he managed to catch himself. If he hurt himself, he didn't let it show as he scurried the rest of the way down. Once he hit the ground, he pelted toward me. Seeing he was going for the bag, I grabbed it and held it out to him.

"What's wrong?" I asked as he snatched it away from me.

"Run," he said. "Stay right behind me and keep pace."

Without another word of explanation, he turned and took off. My heart pumped hard and I kept close to him. The ground vibrated, but not like an earthquake. It was as though something slammed into the dirt again and again. When Vincent started to slow, I did as well, but if anything, the vibrations became stronger and the thuds and sounds of falling trees were louder.

Vincent stopped, and I did the same, but every particle of me said to run farther.

"We're okay here," Vincent said after watching my gaze dart from one thing to another.

I looked at him, worried, and he pointed up. It wasn't a flower top above us. Instead, it looked like giant spokes coming out from a fat white stem.

The ground jolted so hard I almost fell over. I'm not sure what he saw in my face, but he walked past me, and then motioned for me to come with him. He brought me to a small open place, where nothing blocked the view from ground to sky.

Or what passed as a sky.

He nodded back the way we'd come. Another thump sounded and a giant creature came into view. However, this wasn't a giant like the Lost we had back at home. This was a furry creature, its tan coat mottled with color. It bounded forward and the ground shook each time it landed.

My breath caught. The animal was larger than my house, yet when it twitched its nose and bent over, coming back up chewing on fresh greenery, I couldn't help but think it was adorable. I watched for a while, seeing another bound by not too far beyond the first.

Both had large circular golden-brown eyes that glinted in the bright light. I could have watched them all day.

Smiling, I glanced back to Vincent, only to find he wasn't next to me. He leaned against a mushroom stem several yards away, watching every move I made.

"I thought you'd like those." It was a nice sentiment said with no emotion.

It didn't ruin my good mood. "I do," I said, looking back at them. The vibrations died as the creatures went on their way.

I didn't need to sense him to know he was glad he'd shown me.

"We should move on," Vincent said.

"Sure. Right behind you."

There were still beautiful petals soaring above us, but the farther we went the more the mushrooms began to crowd everything else out. After seeing the cute animals, I felt lighter. Sadly, even the short run to avoid the creatures left me tired again.

"Can we stop for a break soon?" I asked.

At first, I thought he shook his head, but then he seemed to spot something. "Over here, though we can't take much time."

He moved toward three flowers growing closely together, providing a large expanse of coverage on one side.

I sat down and leaned against the plant. The small hairs provided a soft cushion. It was the closest thing to comfort I'd felt since we arrived here, and it was impossible not to close my eyes for a few minutes.

"I'll grab some caffeine for you," Vincent said.

"Thanks," I said, not opening my eyes. "I forget how many are left. If I take two is there some for later?"

"There's only two. Go ahead and keep hold of both so you don't need to wait for me to hand them over later."

I sighed, then opened my eyes. Something above me caught my attention, but I had a hard time focusing on it. It looked like an overly large ball with wires stringing it up.

"What's that?" I asked.

Vincent stopped digging through the bag and looked my way. "Oh shit! Cass, get away!"

There was a high-pitched shriek and the wires broke free, falling down, surrounding me. Then, trailing behind, a sphere hurdled toward me.

I screamed and slid straight into the Path. A solid shell formed above me a split-second before the previously camou-flaged body struck.

At the bottom of the creature was a circle. When it screeched again the mouth opened wide, showing jaggedly sharp razors. The beast lifted itself and slammed its body down again. It bounced much like the ball I'd mistaken it for. When it landed again, I got a closer look at rows and rows of teeth behind the first set. I closed my eyes to avoid seeing the horror, but that only succeeded in shutting out my natural sight. The Path still lit the monstrosity...

Which was being swallowed.

The creature's Path was absorbed by darkness, and when I

opened my eyes I saw the animal wither away, as did the flowers around us.

I stared, too afraid to move as petals crashed to the ground.

"Damnit, Cass, let me through." A shade pushed against my cage and I almost screamed again, but my normal sight overrode my initial reaction. It was Vincent.

As soon as I released my protection he grabbed me and dragged me away. Shaking, I watched the consuming dark spread out, killing more flowers. Mushrooms started falling apart.

Vincent dropped me flat onto the ground without any warning, but I didn't complain. Vincent, not bothering with being gentle on my account, started checking my clothes, running his hands over them and around their edges.

"Did anything touch you or drip on you?" Vincent barked, but then he slowed his movements.

He must have found his answer.

Being more delicate, he pulled me to him and gripped me in a hug. He didn't squeeze, but each of his muscles was tight, as though restraining themselves from crushing me. I closed my eyes and tried to relax; when I did, I realized I wasn't the only one shaking. Before I had the chance to second guess myself, I wrapped my arms around Vincent and hugged him back.

Our breathing rasped as though we'd run several miles, but as we calmed down, mine became less labored. After a few minutes it finally returned to some semblance of normalcy. When I relaxed again, adrenaline tried to call my tab and settle up. I was more tired than I had been before we stopped.

Depression attempted to move in as well. "You were right," I said. "It's too hard to keep me alive here. I wouldn't blame you if you walked away."

"That's not funny, Cass."

Thinking of the spider-like creature again, a chill went through me. "That doesn't make it any less true."

He kept one arm around me, staying in contact. "Nothing is going to stop me from taking you out of here." He released me and stood up. When he offered, I took his hand and let him help me to my feet. There was a new resolve written across his face.

And it was penned in black. Vincent's eyes were flat black, and streaks ran up and down his face and neck.

"Give me a minute to take care of things here, and we'll go," Vincent said.

I wasn't sure what he meant by 'take care of things,' since everything was already dead. I ruffled through the bag and took a pain pill. When I looked around, Vincent appeared to be meditating. Not wanting to disturb him, I went over to the flowers I had been sitting under, what was left of them anyway. There was no way to distinguish what they once were.

"You shouldn't stay in that area too long," Vincent said.

There didn't seem to be anything dangerous around. "Why not?"

When I turned to him, he looked normal once again. My Vincent.

My heart spasmed at the thought. He wasn't really mine. I had to stop thinking about him that way if I was going to get through this.

"There's no way of knowing its safe," Vincent said. "Besides, we need to go."

Without really thinking about it, I stepped into the Path. The flow in the area was back to normal. No hint of the darkness lingered.

"We're going this way," Vincent said. It was a subtle prod to get me moving.

Before I wasted any more energy, I stepped out of the Path and once again followed Vincent.

We traveled for what seemed like hours. Around us the flowers dwindled in number, and then disappeared altogether, leaving only mushrooms and some scrubby ground covering behind.

The fungus appeared to become smaller. I couldn't say why, but it was unsettling.

"Are you okay?" Vincent asked.

"Tired," I admitted. "Exhausted, really."

"But not injured?"

"No more than I was before."

He didn't say anything for a while, and I regretted my choice of words.

My head now reached the height of the mushrooms. When my stomach squirmed, I realize the source of my discomfort— it was the change in scale. Logically, I knew we weren't growing taller, though it felt that way.

"It's been a long time since I've brought someone into this world," Vincent said. "Someone I wanted to keep alive, I mean."

There was a completely irrational squirm of jealousy. "Who did you bring over before?"

It took him a while to answer. "It was a friend of mine. Eva's fiancé. Former fiancé, that is. He's deceased."

My head now rose over the mushrooms and I put my hand across my stomach, wanting my insides to settle down. Mentioning it wasn't a good idea, though. Vincent was in the mood to talk, and I wanted to take advantage of that.

"You've mentioned him before," I said. "Did you bring him over to show him this place?"

"We came here before he met Eva. The first time, he goaded

me into it." A touch of warmth entered Vincent's voice. "It took me a while, because I wanted to make sure my sister was nearby. He was really interested in what could be found between worlds."

"He drew the painting hanging in your living room, didn't he?"

"That's right. When we made it home the first time, Eva was livid. It was the first time they met. She told both of us off before storming away. It was love at first sight for him. Not long after that, all three of us started traveling here."

"How were you all getting home if Eva was here?"

"My sister is far more talented than me when it comes to crossing from our world and back again, she's the one that brought us back and forth. She said she came with us to make sure we could get out when we needed. She loved it though. We all did."

"What did you all do?"

"Everything," Vincent said, sounding wistful. "Eva and I always treated this place as a nightmare. But when there were three of us, it was an adventure."

"I wish I could have seen that," I said.

"We were stupid," Vincent said, and the lightness in his voice died. "After he died, Eva came back with me once. The magic was gone. Once again, there were only nightmares."

"But you kept coming," I said after he didn't continue.

He shook his head. "You still don't understand."

Normally I would have bristled at the statement, but I felt too sick to be bothered by it.

"I'm the biggest nightmare here," he continued. "This is where I belong."

"You say that about yourself, but I know you wouldn't say that about your sister."

He stopped and turned on me, glaring. "My sister is *nothing* like me. She walks from one side to the other. Nothing else. She belongs in your world."

"*Our* world," I corrected, then covered my mouth for fear of getting sick.

"What's wrong?" Vincent asked, his words still marred with anger.

I swallowed hard and breathed deeply from my nose a few times. "Nothing. Let's go."

When I moved on, I noticed the forest ahead.

Vincent fell behind, but after a while caught up and took the lead once again. He stayed closer to me than he had previously, especially when the light began to fade.

The mushrooms continued to shrink until the largest ones didn't even make it up to my knees. I was beginning to think they weren't the reason I felt sick.

It's probably this world. I don't belong here.

"Can we navigate the forest at night?" I asked.

"It's not night," Vincent said. It sounded like an automatic response. He seemed to be thinking of something else.

"In the dark, then," I snapped. "Is it going to be difficult to get through with the flare going out?"

"It's an inopportune time, but we'll be okay. There's enough light to get through."

"I'm going to need to rest soon." I hated to say it, but I had to.

"We'll stop at the edge of the forest. It'll be safer under some of the younger trees."

We came to a wide expanse of open area. Now that the mushrooms were normal in size, I felt exposed.

Luckily, the emptiness didn't last long. Trees began to dot the landscape.

Vincent soon stopped and dropped his bag. I leaned

against the tree and watched him rummage through our supplies.

Leaning wasn't enough, so I gave up and sat cross-legged and rested my forehead in my hands. When Vincent came over, I didn't look up. It was interesting to note, however, that he walked around the tree slowly, as though inspecting it, and I could hear him running his hands over areas of the trunk.

He must have been satisfied with what he found, because he sat down next to me.

"I have something for your stomach," he said. "First, though, I need you to look up, so I can check some things."

Frowning, I sat up. "What do you need?"

Before the words were out, he gripped my chin and stared into my eyes. He'd done it before, but only when trying to get a feel for my soul.

"What are you doing?" I asked.

"I should have kept you out of the blighted ground I created," he said. "I need to get an idea of any damage it may have caused."

I rolled my eyes. "The area wasn't 'blighted.' Trust me, I've seen that kind of thing. You didn't leave anything behind."

Small creases appeared around his eyes. Again, I couldn't help but wonder if I really saw them. Back home even Rider and Logan noticed nothing.

No. I saw what I wanted to.

"You can't be sure of that," Vincent said.

I shrugged. "The Path doesn't lie."

"But there have been Paths that you couldn't see."

He was being difficult, so I pulled away and put my head back in my hands, staring down into my lap. "I'm pretty sure Logan was right. I think that was another Reader. Besides, I saw the Path you created. It's gone."

"Look up again," he said.

I sighed loudly, but lifted my head.

This time, he didn't hold my face, but he put his hand against my forehead, then cheeks, before handing me two pills and some water.

"This is going to go well on top of the caffeine," I mumbled.

"When was the last time you ate?" Vincent asked.

"I don't know. Did we have a power bar before we got here?"

Vincent shook his head and grabbed something from his bag. "That was days ago. No wonder you aren't feeling well."

"I'm not hungry," I said. "Have you eaten anything?"

"I'll eat when we get back."

"But you--"

"I don't need food here," Vincent said, handing me a protein bar. "Usually, it's not even an option. It's not like I have a chance to pack a bag, and I'm not eating anything from this place."

I picked at the food, eating about half before I stowed it in my pocket.

"You should eat the whole thing," Vincent said.

I shrugged and put my head back down.

"We shouldn't stay long," Vincent said, standing up. "But rest while you can."

Vincent moved around; sometimes he went far enough away that I couldn't hear him, but he was always back before I started to worry. While I sat my stomach began to feel better, leaving only tiredness in its place.

"Do you want to grab another drink before we go?" Vincent asked.

I nodded and dragged myself to my feet before taking the proffered bottle. Looking around, I saw what light we had been left with. Although the flare was gone, everything around seemed to glow.

A blue cloud floated nearby. It wasn't moving, but looking closer I saw currents flowed inside. For some reason, it raised my spirits, although I couldn't say for sure why. Maybe because it was brighter than everything else, or prettier. Either way, I felt lighter.

I passed the bottle back to Vincent and stretched before we moved on. As the forest grew denser it also turned darker, but there was still enough light to keep me from tripping over debris.

"We're going to avoid the center of the woods," Vincent said. "It'll take us off track."

"What's wrong with that area?" I asked.

After I asked the question, I heard a whisper next to me. I froze for a moment but saw nothing out of the ordinary.

"The deeper we go, the worse things get," Vincent said. "I wish we could circle farther around and stay in the young woods, but I don't think we can take that kind of time."

Over Vincent's last few words, I once again heard an odd whisper. When I turned, I saw the blue cloud drifted behind us.

Is it following us? It lifted my spirits, so I was glad to see it, but I wasn't sure how I felt about it tracking us.

"What lives in here?" I asked, slowing down. Out of the corner of my eyes I saw a shape in the trees. Startled, my head whipped around, but there was nothing. Only the tree trunk.

"Aside from the trees, not much. Sometimes animals stray into the forest, but if they survive they don't stay long."

"Survive what?" I cast a nervous glance at the cloud, wondering if it was actually something I should be leery of. Once again, when I looked askance I saw a shape—smaller than the first, but definitely there. I tried to keep it in sight as I turned slowly, but it was gone.

CHAPTER

SEVEN

Vincent stopped and waited for me to move up beside him. "Stay very still and listen."

When I did, Vincent's steady breath and my own raspy one were loudly apparent. Then the whispers started—louder this time.

"I heard those while we were walking," I said. "And I've been seeing something too, out of the corner of my eye. What is it?"

Vincent frowned and studied the forest around us. The noise died away.

"You should walk next to me," Vincent said, taking my hand.

"What is it?" I repeated.

"The trees. They usually aren't so talkative, and ones this age never show themselves. The deeper we go, the more you'll see and hear. Remember what I said before. Don't listen to them. They'll tell you all sorts of things, but do your best to ignore them."

"I can see the trees," I said, trying to understand. "What else is here?"

"These are not the kind of plants we have in our world. As these grow older they gain a basic sentience and can spread themselves beyond their own trunk. When they leave they aren't solid and they're still attached to the wood in some way, but they aren't completely inside their physical shape."

"Why is it when I look straight at them, they're gone?"

"Not gone, they're just not seen. And these shouldn't be this lively. It might be better if we go wider around and avoid older trees."

The sounds started to make me nervous. I couldn't make out any of the whispers, but the forms were there from time to time in my peripheral vision.

When I glanced behind, the blue misty form hovered. "And what's that behind us?"

"Almost nothing in this world has been studied," Vincent said, turning. "That is... a shiny cloud. We've seen them between flares. It wasn't there when we passed, but they can appear seemingly from nowhere. They've never hurt anyone, and it's definitely not something we need to be worried about right now."

"It's following us."

Vincent sighed. "They don't follow people—you're just seeing another one. They come and go. We should focus on the trees, and make a plan."

I didn't like his dismissal. "What are our options? To go deeper into the woods, which gets us home faster, or go around. How much longer will it take?"

"In our world, it'll add about an extra two days to our travel--maybe more."

My heart sunk. "And how far away are we now?"

"Distance isn't really—" He stopped when he saw the exasperated look on my face. The corner of his lip curled up. "Around a day and half, maybe two."

My shoulders sagged. "I'm guessing either way we're not going to have a chance to sleep."

"In about--I don't know, thirteen, fourteen hours--we'll find a spot to rest for a few minutes. That's if we take the short way."

I stared at him, not able to fully comprehend what he said.

"But that place is not here," Vincent said. "We need to press on."

"The shorter way, right?" I asked.

"We'll try it."

Vincent tried to set a brisk pace, but I was out of steam. I plodded along behind him, barely noticing anything. Eventually, the whispers seeped into my brain, digging in and taking root.

"How do you do this?" I asked.

"It's easier for me," Vincent said. "I wish I could make it easier for you, but I'm doing the best I can."

"It only takes you a week to get to your sister's when you disappear back home. We were so much closer when we arrived, so shouldn't we have made it already?" I hated myself for asking, because I was getting dangerously close to whining. It didn't help that my stomach started to twist and my head ached.

Vincent rubbed his head and kept walking. "Distances don't work the same way here as they do for other places. If this piece of ground we're standing on led to our world, it could just as easily take us to Greenland as it could Utah."

I clutched my stomach and didn't try to comprehend. The forest grew darker around us, and the voices became loud enough to make out the actual words spoken. Warnings of danger ahead came from every side.

"Also," he added after a while, "when I travel, I usually go directly from point A and B."

"We're taking the scenic route?" I asked.

"You could say that."

Words slammed together in my head, but I couldn't get them to line up through the anger. Out of nowhere, a soothing sensation rolled over me. Looking around to find the source, I realized the blue cloud caught up. It surrounded me like a happy streak of the Path and seeped straight into my veins.

My illness died and I was more awake than I had been since leaving oasis.

"We can't stay here," Vincent said. "Look, we traveled the way I thought would be best." A moment later he sighed. "We have to move on." He sounded terse, but I didn't care.

To be honest, I hadn't even noticed I'd stopped.

When he turned, he stared at me a few moments before rubbing his forehead and closing his eyes. "Of course. Even the clouds want to see you."

That stung.

Whispers changed, urging him to leave me, while others still warned of danger.

Vincent did seem mildly curious about my predicament, because he moved closer to me. The haze of blue shifted between us and Vincent stopped just shy of the cloud.

"I know you're upset," Vincent said. "But you shouldn't be using your power. You'll only wear yourself out."

I closed my eyes and breathed deeply. "I'm not reading." Thoughts of being furious with Vincent dwindled, making room for contentment.

"I took us this way for a reason." He was getting angrier, but there was a pleading note to his voice. "We couldn't have survived the other way."

Some of the peace fled with his words. It felt as though he

cracked my heart open. "Because it's too hard to keep me alive?"

"Going the other way, it would have been."

Any happy feelings fell aside. The blue mist shifted away from me, but kept itself between me and Vincent.

"That came out wrong," Vincent said. "Had we gone from where we started, straight to my sister, the chance of losing you would have been too high."

Once again, the full weight of the burden I was fell on me like a lead weight. "And then the elf would give you hell. And Rider... you just can't win here, can you."

The chorus of voices chimed in, agreeing. I couldn't tell exactly where the sound came from, but more and more of them wanted him to leave me behind.

Vincent rubbed his forehead again. "Can you please drop this barrier? We can talk as we walk."

"I'm not reading. I told you that already."

"Things seem to work different here," Vincent mumbled. "Maybe you just need to calm down."

My eyes narrowed. "Excuse me?"

"We have to move," he finally snapped.

I walked through the cloud, glaring at him until I passed him. "Why don't you just wait for the monsters to come? You can let them take care of me, and then you can go home."

He didn't say anything, and for a while I ended up in the lead again. Not that I knew where I was going, or cared. It had been a mistake to say what I did. Not only was it purposefully cruel, but it also gave the trees fodder and the words they whispered turned darker.

With the cloud gone my stomach twisted enough without the trees telling me I was a burden. They tried to convince me Vincent would kill me to make it easier on himself, but I didn't believe that.

Of course, wasn't that what accused him of?

The woods grew dimmer, for which my furiously aching head appreciated. It was almost too dark to see, but I kept going.

Right up to the point the screaming started.

I stopped dead. They were heart-wrenching screams of agony broken with pleas of help.

"Come this way," Vincent said dully.

"Someone's in trouble." I said, although I wasn't quite sure it was true.

"It's the trees. We went too deep and need to circle around."

"Those are trees?" I'm not sure when I started shaking, but if anything, it made me feel even sicker. "Are they trying to trick us into searching for someone?"

He started walking on, albeit slowly. "No. This is what it sounds like when you get to the older part of the forest."

"Why?" I followed him, still looking deeper into the darkness.

"Because they're eating each other."

I clapped my hand over my mouth, trying not to lose what little I had eaten.

"It's survival of the fittest between the worlds," Vincent said without prompting. "The strong takes what they want from the weak."

Survival of the fittest? I really hate this place.

I didn't ask any more questions as we walked, and I was relieved when the screams died away. I knew those cries of anguish would haunt my dreams.

"When we get back," Vincent said, breaking our long silence, "if you want me to leave, you're going to have to say it."

His words came out of nowhere, taking me by surprise. It took me a while to find my voice. "Is that what you want?"

"I think it's what you want, but I have to hear it from you. Not here, but once we're back home. If you still feel the same way, you're going to have to tell me."

"I'm sure things will be fine once we've had some rest."

When he didn't say anything, I began to worry.

"Don't you think so?" I asked.

He didn't answer right away, which allowed room for the voices to pick up once again. They dug into my head, pulling out words that hurt.

"At some point in this hell, something broke between us," Vincent said. "It was something bad enough that you closed yourself off from me."

"You don't need another distraction from me," I said.

"That's why you did it?" Vincent turned on me, radiating outrage.

The trees picked up a chorus of admonishments. I looked around behind us, wanting to find the source. It had to be something they did when they stretched away from their trunks. If I found even one of them, I was sure I could get them to stop.

Vincent appeared in front of me, seemingly from nowhere. His icy fingers brushed my face and I stepped back, instantly getting a chill.

"We need to work on our communication skills," he said, though his voice was soft again.

"What communication skills?" I asked.

"That's exactly my point." He put his hand against my fore-head and I pushed it away. "What's this?" he asked while pulling at my shirt and examining my neck.

"What are you doing?" I snapped.

The trees mocked and taunted until I couldn't help but search again for a source.

"Cass, look at me," Vincent said.

When I did, he only received a glare.

"Stop listening to them."

"How?" I put my hands over my ears, in an effort to block the sound, but it stopped nothing. "They're so loud, and there's so many of them."

Vincent wrapped his arm around mine and started to lead me onward. "How many are talking to you?"

All around me, they snickered and told me Vincent was patronizing me and he didn't really care.

"All of them," I said.

"Listen to me," he said. "You're sick. I'm not sure what happened, but you're running a high fever. We're away from the older trees now, so what you're hearing isn't really there."

"Why do you keep doing that?" I asked.

"What?"

"I say something and you dismiss it out of hand. I tell you I'm not reading and you ignore me. I tell you these trees are saying way more than you seem to think, yet you brush it aside."

"Your power works differently here, is all," Vincent said. "I was trying to make you see that."

"You're not listening to me. I may as well not even be here." I tried to push away from him, but my head began to spin and I was forced to lean on him instead.

Vincent stopped and gripped me tight. He stared behind us for more than a minute.

"We need to move," he said. "Faster."

"And then there's that," I snapped. "You want to talk about lack of communication, so why don't we start there. Is something following us or not?"

"I really don't want to worry you."

I closed my eyes and rubbed my head, wanting to scream or cry.

Maybe both.

"Whatever," I mumbled, knowing the word would aggravate the hell out of him.

"You are unbelievably irritating," he said.

"I wouldn't know what that feels like, would I?"

He sighed. "It's possible someone is following me."

"You?" I asked. "Not us?"

"Not us," he agreed. "I told you, I'm the monster here." He sounded sad, which squeezed my heart. "There are always people who go after monsters."

"You're saying people hunt Walkers in this world?"

"In every world," Vincent said. "But between the worlds, taking down a Walker can earn someone a good bounty."

"What do we do?" I asked.

"We're almost out of the woods. I was hoping we could reach our destination ahead of them, but we're not close enough. And we can't move faster."

"Sorry," I said, knowing I was the cause of all this grief.

He hugged me to him for a moment. "It's not your fault. I should have dealt with it already, but I wanted to spare you that."

"Spare me what?"

"Actually," he sighed. "That's not exactly the truth."

"Are you trying to muddle my thoughts?" My head was already foggy and I felt like throwing up. The conversation wasn't helping.

"It wasn't my intention. I didn't want you to see who I am, or what I do to people. Although, I think I'm too late on that account. That's what happened, isn't it? What I can't remember--what I'm not letting myself remember. I did something."

"Do you mean like what you did to the spider thing?"

"No." He paused and I could feel his confusion "If I had

done something, you'd know what I was talking about. If that's not what pushed you away, what was it? Did I hurt you?"

Why couldn't we be home already? "You just... said some things. Is it important now?"

"Important?" Vincent sounded incredulous. He didn't yell, but wisps of muddy green light steamed off him and quickly dissipated. "You've cut a gaping hole in me!"

Not believing what I saw, I closed my eyes, trusting him to guide us. "You're being overly dramatic."

"You have *no* idea. No understanding of what you did." His voice seethed and he took a deep breath reigning in his emotion. "The spark of light you created went out. All the emotion that spilled from you, happiness, sadness, pain, anger--everything. It's gone now. And what's even worse, you won't tell me why."

His anger pushed me around, making me cringe. When I opened my eyes, the world spun, so I closed them again. I began to sweat profusely and my muscles turned watery.

And more upsetting, I had trouble figuring out to say that wouldn't make things worse.

"Can this conversation wait?" I asked.

Vincent expelled air in an angry huff.

"Fine," I snapped. I tried to stand a little straighter, but it didn't work. I leaned heavily against Vincent and I was too weak to change that. "You told me how you felt, okay."

"You're upset that I love you?"

"No! I'm hurt because you said your life has been straight-up hell since you met me, and you were upset because I was always around."

"I didn't—"

"I'm not done," I snapped, cutting him off. "You said you should have left me when you had the chance and you'd be better off if you had. *That's* why I pulled myself back. I've obviously misunderstood something."

"I don't--"

"And then you wanted to use me as bait for whatever chased us." Tears fell which only made me angrier. "You said if I bled, I'd attract even more of them." Vincent drew back, which left me unbalanced. "You wanted to deal with them all at once. You said everyone would believe me dying here was an accident." I started to breathe heavier, and since I stopped sweating, I was chilled. It might as well have been winter.

"You know I didn't mean that, right? You know none of it is true."

"Words like those don't come from nowhere." My thoughts became distorted, and I lost track of what I was saying. Oddly enough, Zander popped into my head. "I had to break myself off before it hurt any worse."

"We're almost to a place where you can rest," Vincent said in a wary voice. "I'll make this right, but... I don't know how."

"Something's wrong." For some reason I thought it needed to be said.

"I know. We have to talk about this, but we're out of time."

"No. I mean..." Putting one foot in front of the other became more difficult, and following a train of thought was becoming impossible. "I'm... not well."

Vincent stopped and tried to hold me up and look at me at the same time. "What is this?" he asked, pulling on the neck of my shirt again. He traced a line from my collarbone to my chest.

"I need to sit. Or something."

He scanned the area and didn't move, but didn't let me rest either.

"Over here," he said, more to himself than me.

We started moving, but then I blinked it was as though

time jumped. I looked around, and nothing looked familiar. The world twisted, becoming distorted and I closed my eyes again to avoid the unnatural movements. Another leap in time and Vincent was settling me onto the ground.

I thought laying down would help, but no such luck. Soon he hauled me back up to a sitting position. My limbs ached and worked about as well as a rag doll.

He gave me more pills. My nose scrunched up, but I took them. The water felt like liquid life and I sucked it all down.

The drink revived me. "Is there any more water?"

"We have one bottle left, but there's still a long way to go. It might be best to save some."

He focused back the way we had come and studied our trail for what seemed like ages.

"Are you seeing the blue cloud again?" I asked after a while. "That would help." I laid down, not bothering to search for it myself. The idea had been wishful thinking.

He smiled down on me. "If I could bring you a cloud, I would." He glanced away again. "I need you to stay here and get some sleep, okay?"

"That doesn't sound safe."

"I'm going to take care of a problem and I'll be gone for a short while. If you lay down and stay still, you should be fine."

I closed my eyes, just happy with not needing to move. "As long as I'm not bait."

"Never," Vincent said. He brushed hair away from my face. "I know you don't believe me, but I hope you will when you're better. I'll do what I can to fix this, but right now I have to go."

He gave me a quick kiss and disappeared. I thought about turning to watch him go—or to at least figure out which way he went. Instead, I fell asleep.

Naturally, I had nightmares and fever dreams. Noises

nearby woke me. I blinked, but didn't move. When I glanced around I saw someone approaching, and it wasn't Vincent.

A man leaned over me. The moment I tried to cry out something foul filled my mouth, making it hard to breathe, much less make any noise.

When I bit down there was no obvious effect. I tried to kick or hit, but somehow, I was already bound. Some sort of rough rope was wrapped all around me. When it pulled tight, I involuntarily tried to scream, but gagged and choked.

A thick, almost chunky liquid began to creep down my throat. My stomach churned in disgust. With my oxygen cut off my sight dimmed, then died.

CHAPTER

EIGHT

S ounds of revelry filtered in then fell away, only to come back again. My skin felt bruised from head to toe, which was nothing compared to my insides. Without opening my eyes or moving, I tried to take stock of the situation.

On the plus side, I was alive. At least I thought it was a positive. My arms were tied behind my back, my feet were bound, and I laid on the ground face first. A foul taste in my mouth repulsed me and I felt on fire inside and out.

Noises continued to fade in and out. Only a few voices sounded distinct, so maybe it wasn't a large event, but it was definitely a celebration.

"She's up!" someone shouted excitedly. Another person said something I didn't understand and I was dragged to a sitting position.

My sight went in and out of focus, so I closed my eyes tight and willed them to work. When I opened them again every-thing was still blurry, though it was a little better than before.

More than a few people stood around, and I heard others talking behind me.

"She's sick," someone said. "That might drive the price down."

"Price?" I tried to ask, but no sound came with the words. My voice wasn't coarse or croaky. It was gone.

"I already told you, we aren't selling her," someone snapped. A hard-looking person came into view. His face was rough and stony with a number of what could have been scars covering it. He came closer. "Her and her friend killed members of our tribe."

"A person, even a damaged one, catches too high of a price to just kill her."

A few other people said something, but it was unintelligible—in a language I had never heard.

I tried to tell them to go to hell, but only a hint of sound escaped.

"I've thought about that," the man said. "That's why we sell her a little at a time, on an as-needed basis."

A conversation quickly picked up around me. I didn't understand the language, but it sounded as though there were at least four voices aside from two men that spoke my language.

It didn't matter what they said. I was getting out of there.

"The Walker can't find her," the man snapped. "Even if he survived, there's no way for him to find us. Unless someone screwed up."

I almost smiled. Vincent would track me anywhere. He always knew what was happening and always turned up. All through the bond we shared.

The one that I cut off.

Mentally I ranted at myself for a few moments before

turning inward. I needed to embrace Vincent again. There was a problem of trust I had to get over, but it was a small obstacle.

If I broke down my walls blocking Vincent, he'd be able to find me.

"Let's take a look," a man said, looming over me.

I hadn't noticed anyone approach and I started.

He grabbed me by the arm and yanked me to my feet. A fresh wave of nausea and pain swept over me.

"Keep her legs and arms tied tight, but loosen the rest. We need to see what we have."

I started to shake. Ignoring the man holding me, and the two that joined him, I closed my eyes and reached for Vincent —which did very little. It wasn't like reaching for the Path.

Instead, I thought of everything I loved about him. When something sharp rubbed across my arm, I ignored it. When pain radiated along my scalp, I kept my eyes shut. None of it mattered. As soon as I re-opened myself to Vincent, I'd take care of them.

All of them.

As I thought of waking up next to Vincent—his smile, and all the wonderful moments we captured together— something loosened inside me. I loved him, truly loved him. Head over heels.

Something pierced my leg, which was harder to ignore, but my mind was still tied to Vincent and I reached out, trying to sense him.

When they grabbed my mouth and forced it open, my concentration snapped.

"Your brother tried to use her as a pollinator before he died. We need her to survive it or she's worthless."

I glared at the three of them around me. One appeared vaguely human, another was human shaped, but his skin was a dark green color that I'd never seen on any Lost. The last one looked very much like a tree.

My eyes narrowed. This must be the brother to the leshen that grabbed me when I first arrived. It bothered me that he looked pleasant and peaceful.

Either Vincent was on his way or he wasn't. It didn't matter anymore. I was done with these people.

The man let go of my face. He must have seen a hint of what I planned when he looked into my eyes and stepped back.

"Tighten the restraints again and throw her down. We'll drug her and travel farther."

The ropes around me bit painfully into my skin and I fell hard to the ground. Still, I forced myself to sit up and look around.

For a moment I worried someone in the area might be innocent, but I quickly dismissed the idea. If they weren't bound like me, then this was a choice for them, and I saw no other prisoners.

There were around eleven. Most were humanoid. There were a few green, like one of the first three, another had skin that faded from light to dark purple and had spots reminiscent of a cheetah.

I stared at one figure longer than the others. It was dark, more like a shadow than a person, but I sensed that there was life inside the form.

Someone stepped into my line of sight and sneered at me. The leader said something to the man that I didn't understand.

The man spoke harsh words to the leader and the leader laughed. "She'll do whatever work she's told to do. If she causes too much trouble, we'll sell her outright. Either way, we win."

These weren't people, and it was easy for me to convince

myself of that. It didn't matter what their races were. They weren't even animals. These were true monsters.

Every particle of my being hurt, but I tried to push it aside as much as I could. Thankfully when I drifted into the Path, some of the pain dulled.

Deciding what to do didn't take time. There was only one thing I could do to ensure these people wouldn't take me anywhere. It would take repeating the worst thing I had ever done—something I had never wanted to do until meeting these monstrous people.

The leader--or at least the one giving orders--watched me. The others gathered belongings, getting ready to leave. My eyes hardened into a glare, but I smiled. I really really wanted to say something, though I knew any sound I made would be meaningless.

I'm not sure what the leader expected, but I could see his attitude shifting—a seed of doubt sprouted.

"Load up," he barked. "Knock her out and let's go."

The moment I heard someone approach, I put a barrier around myself. One of the green men walked straight into the invisible wall. He pressed it a few times, testing. It was obvious he had no idea what it was. Confused, he waved over a man who could have been his twin they looked so much alike.

I watched the two while I prepared to do something I swore to myself I'd never do again. Pulling together a fine razor-sharp stream of air was easier than I thought it would be. I had to make sure it was fine, but sharp and strong enough to rip through flesh and bone.

A green puff of what I began to assume was Path floated nearby. It made me second guess what I planned. Was there another way?

No. It was clear these people had done this before and

would do it again. They had looked me over and knew what kind of price they could get.

I shivered at the thought before carefully adjusting what I had prepared, making sure my anger-fueled revenge didn't touch the pure cloud. What I was about to do would contaminate anything good.

Then, watching the leader the whole time, I stretched my creation across the camp. I hesitated once again, but pressed forward before I could think about it much longer. The invisible blade was held tight in my hand as I circled it around above me, making sure to cover as much area as I could.

Camp noises continued for a moment or two longer than I'd expected. Then a heartbeat of silence followed by the sickening sound of people falling apart. It was almost masked by the crash of the trees that had been caught in the crossfire, but nothing could hide the horrendous noise of peoples' insides sliding out.

I dropped my work before I used the last of my strength and tried to keep the self-loathing and doubt off of my face. The leader looked horrified for a minute, then that cruel gleam shone again and he glanced beside me.

When I turned slightly, I saw I missed someone. One of the tree people came into view, causing my nose to curl up in disgust.

How could something so beautiful be so heinous? It was hard to distinguish a face among the bark, but a vindictive, almost gleeful Path rolled from the man.

The two looked far too sure they wouldn't be joining their friends.

I've missed something. While fumbling to create the same weapon of destruction, I twisted, trying to see both men at once.

Roots erupted from the ground and wrapped themselves

tight around my throat. They crushed my airways and latched on wherever they could. They attempted to bore through my skin.

One thought popped into my head. I grabbed the tree's Path and halted it. Stopped it dead. It was as though the thing had been frozen in time.

Beside him, I saw the leader move. Trapping him was almost an afterthought. My concentration was on the leshen.

I stared, unsure of what exactly I had done. No new Path was being created. No emotion, no thoughts. It had stopped making any type of mark on the world.

The only Path left was inside the thing's body, the core of his being.

There was no use for that core anymore. I grabbed it and pulled, but I was met with resistance.

Of course. I wasn't a Walker. If this was the man's soul, it was his. As a Reader, I couldn't take that. Instead, I gave it the same treatment I had given the others. I let go of its Path and it fell into two pieces which I tried not to look at. A part of me assumed I'd see wood fall out of him.

But he was very much a person and I closed my eyes to avoid seeing more than a glance of what fell out of him.

The roots which held me didn't let go. I twisted, but my bindings remained wrapped tightly around my neck and body. I wanted to cry out in frustration, but I could barely breathe.

The idea of what I had done made me ill, and when I opened my eyes the terror on the leader's face etched itself into my mind.

The man started to beg, although when he switched to a different language it was possible he cursed me as well.

The green haze floated over, and I hesitated. Inside the cloud was the Path--I was certain. There were flows and channels of energy which shimmered and rolled over each other in a beautiful flow.

That was what the Path should be. Beautiful--like my tree back home and this cloud. Every time I watched the Path it was a wondrous thing that I wanted to stare at forever.

But then I had touched it, bent it, twisted it, and forced it to do things the Path never should have been used for.

I looked back at the man. He stopped talking and fixated on me. A tiny smirk played on his face.

He had been going to sell me, little by little, and I didn't think he meant cutting me up. I shivered.

Without thinking of it any further, I dropped his containment and cut the man in half. I watched as my creation bit into the flesh. His eyes almost immediately lost focus and dimmed.

He fell without a noise.

It was difficult to look around from my vantage point, but I did my best. I'd caused fear and death here, and I deserved to be plagued with the memory of the horror I caused.

It never should have happened. The only spark of good I could dredge up was the thought that maybe I saved someone else future harm.

Being bound and too weary for anything else, I laid down, focusing exclusively on the cloud floating nearby.

I was exhausted in so many ways. Tired of this world, the pain, the ugliness--everything...especially myself. When I let go of my power, I knew it would only be worse.

A spot of movement under the haze caught my eye. I should have been scared--worried that I'd missed something or someone dangerous--but I was beginning to go numb, and didn't care.

Below the green mass, a chox appeared. Much like the cloud, the Path inside the little animal flowed beautifully.

The chox made a squeaky little bark, then ran away.

Figuring it was the last good thing I would see, I closed my eyes and stepped out of the Path.

I WAS PUSHED OVER ROUGHLY, but too battered to fight back. Each movement caused bouts of pain to radiate through me. Opening my eyes was the best I could manage.

When I did, Vincent brushed the hair from my face. A sense of restrained rage thundered tightly around him. Another emotion hid inside as well, but it was buried and I was too exhausted to dig.

He looked away for a moment, then brought his large knife up to my neck. The binding bit into my flesh as he cut it away. I closed my eyes and gritted my teeth. When the pressure disappeared, I relaxed.

Breathing more deeply caused a fire in my chest, but I was thrilled to get a decent amount of air again.

Vincent chopped away the remaining bindings, none of them hurting as bad as the one around my throat. When he was done, he took my hands and started to work some life into them.

It wasn't until I closed my eyes again that he finally spoke.

"If you can, try to hold off on sleeping," Vincent said.

"Let me guess," I whispered, not opening them. "We can't stop here."

"We can stay if you want," he said. "The blood is going to attract things, but I'll take care of what comes."

My nose curled back. "A little farther it is." The volume of my voice ranged between barely making a sound to a soft whisper. There was nothing louder left inside me.

"Anything broken?" Vincent asked.

I didn't really know, but I shook my head anyway.

Vincent's hands pressed my legs. He gently put pressure in an area before moving to another.

The problem was, it all hurt.

"Stop," I complained.

Vincent yanked his hands back. He seemed to think and I used the time to drift off.

"Okay," Vincent said after a while. "I promise I won't touch you, but I need you to do a few things. You're bleeding and I have to find any other damage."

"What?" Laying down wasn't helping. I obviously had to focus. I reached out my hand to him. "Help me up?"

I thought he was going to refuse, but he took my hand and put an arm around my back. The movement was agony, but once I sat up I didn't feel as bad.

Under the rage he was scared. I sensed that now.

He released me and put a little distance between us.

For some reason that lit a spasm of fear in me. Before he could move too far, I grabbed his hand and tugged him into a hug.

My head laid on his shoulder and I wrapped myself around him. I let one arm fall after a few moments. It wasn't the most comfortable position, but for me nothing was comfortable. For Vincent—

I pulled back in a hurry, and Vincent let go as though scalded. He hadn't said what happened to him and I hadn't asked. I looked him over for any signs of injury.

"What—" I started to say, but no sound came out, so I tried clearing my throat and made a second attempt. "Are you hurt? They thought you wouldn't survive, but no one said..." They were barely words and I couldn't say all that I wanted, but Vincent seemed to understand.

Halfway through, he shook his head. He took my hand and

rubbed it, but looked ready to drop it at the slightest provocation.

"Someone was hired to find me and get me out of the way. I don't think these people cared if I was killed, maimed, or anything else. They just wanted me incapacitated for as long as possible."

"What happened? Were you hurt?"

"I wasn't injured, but she's dead."

"She?"

"Now is not the time for details," Vincent said, sounding stonier than before.

"She?" It came out as a squeak. I pushed myself up straighter and looked around. I couldn't imagine a woman working for these monsters

"Yes." He looked as though he strained to keep calm, but the single word came out hard.

I glared around, seeing parts of the bodies I created from men. "She worked for them." My broken voice couldn't convey my outrage. "I'm glad she died."

Vincent twisted, seeming uncomfortable. "That doesn't sound like you." He reached out to feel my forehead.

I gave him a dirty look. "You don't know what they did." I hated that I couldn't drive the statement with only a ragged whisper. "Or what they planned."

Stay angry, I told myself. *It's easier if I stay angry. Don't think any further.*

"Do you want to tell me?" Vincent asked.

I rolled my eyes and shook my head. "The only thing I want is to go home."

NINE

That wasn't exactly true. I wanted to go home, but even more than that, I wanted to curl up somewhere safe with Vincent. Forever.

"Let's get you on your feet and we can go." Vincent's voice was back to its normal monotone. He passed me pills and water. "It's our last antibiotic and something for the pain. You're still running a fever, but it's not as bad. If I knew what was causing it, I might have a better idea of what you need. How far do the marks run?"

"Where they tied me up? From head to foot."

"Not the bruises. I'm not sure if it's poison or something else, but the veins in your neck are turning dark. It spreads down your chest."

I groaned. That at least came out with a decent amount of noise.

"Check your stomach and side to see how far the lines go and check for puncture wounds."

I lifted up the side of my shirt and noticed for the first time that it was ripped. In fact, it was decorated with tears to the point there was almost nothing left. Memories of the roots jumping up from the ground filled my head and I started to shake. Holes and blood stains covered my jeans as well.

"I'll need your help," I said.

"Are you comfortable with that? If you'd rather, we can try to wait until you can see a doctor," Vincent said.

I rubbed my forehead. "You aren't going to hurt me." I forced a sickly grin. "Actually, I don't think there's any way for me to avoid discomfort. Unless you have a much stronger pain pill hidden away, I'll have to get used to it."

Vincent helped me stand and I took off the shredded remains of my bindings. The cut on my side obviously had him worried.

"This needs stitches," he said. "It's still bleeding."

Dark veins ran down my stomach and spread out and around, covering my back.

"I'm not just sick, am I?" I asked.

"We'll get you to a doctor, they'll be able to help," Vincent said.

I raised an eyebrow at him as he went through our meager supplies. "You know what this is? It's not going to kill me?"

"I found some butterfly closures. That'll save us time on stitches."

"I guess that's my answer." I didn't have to say it under my breath, since nothing could come out above a whisper.

"It had to be the dog bite," Vincent said. "I've just never seen one do this. But nothing else has bitten you, and you haven't consumed anything that would hurt you."

Thinking back, I thought about our first few hours stuck here. When we first arrived and the leshen captured me, something foul had been shoved in my mouth. To get me here, they'd done the same thing, and I remembered a caustic substance working its way down my throat.

"You remember something?" Vincent asked.

The idea was disgusting, and I shook my head automatically. They had said the leshen turned me into a pollinator and hoped I would survive.

"You need to tell me."

"Can we go now?"

"If you know, then there might be something I could do."

The thought was horrific, and I *really* didn't want to put words to it.

"Fine," I squeaked. "We can talk, but we have to go."

Vincent looked as though he wanted to argue, but instead he shoved our now meager supplies away.

I pulled at my clothes, trying to cover the ghastly marks, but the side had been ripped and the front had more holes than could be covered.

"Take mine," Vincent said, already pulling his shirt off.

I pressed my lips hard together and tried not to tear up. It was a simple gesture, but such a sweet one.

After I changed clothes, I wrapped my arms around him.

He patted me gently. "If there's anything else I can do, please ask me, and..." Uncertainty flitted across his features.

"And?" I prompted almost silently.

"Don't shut yourself off to me while we're here. Not again."

The words pulled at my heart and I squeezed him tighter. It took me a while to voice a reply.

"I promise," I said as I pulled away. That and a small smile were the best I could manage.

"We can talk about it again when you're feeling better."

Vincent pointed us in a direction. The whole time we walked through the woods he held my hand in his or kept his arm wrapped around me.

It wasn't until we were away from the horrible trees that I told Vincent what had happened. I gave a very brief version, however. The was no reason to tell him everything they said, and my voice wasn't fit to say much. Besides, with each step I felt worse.

Finally, I had to call for a break, and there was no, 'a little further' this time. I sunk straight down, though I had meant to stay sitting since I wasn't sure I'd be able to get back up.

Somehow, that got lost in translation and I ended up flat on the ground, where I closed my eyes.

"Where are we?" I asked.

"We're close," Vincent said. "As soon as we cross over, we're taking you to the hospital."

"Can they even help? We need an AIR doctor, or maybe MyTH."

"Don't worry. There's a place nearby that takes special cases. My sister will take you straight there."

"Us," I corrected.

Vincent settled in beside me. "I'm not someone you're going to want to be around when I get back."

"I'll always want you around."

"My sister will keep an eye on you. I'll call Logan, too."

"Oh my god, your sister." I blinked my eyes until I was able to keep them open, then tried to sit up, but Vincent pushed me back down.

"What about her?" Vincent asked.

"I can't meet her like this."

He looked at me as though I lost my mind. "That's the last thing you need to think about."

I shook my head and closed my eyes again.

"Rest," Vincent said.

Despite the hard ground it wasn't difficult to fall asleep. When I woke, I felt a little better and sat up. The bag was right next to me, but not Vincent.

My heart seized. I scanned the open space around us. It

wasn't until I looked behind me that I saw Vincent. I grabbed my chest and took a shuddering breath.

He sat only a few yards away and appeared to be meditating. I wasn't going to bother him, but there was a haze building between us. When I tried to find the source, I saw that it circled me.

Whatever it was, it made me uneasy.

"Vincent," I called. My voice was louder than a whisper for the first time in a long while.

Whether he heard something in my voice or sensed my anxiety though our newly re-opened link, I wasn't sure. But I saw him open his eyes and carefully stand.

"What is this?" I asked

"Cass," Vincent said, not taking his eyes off the haze. He backed up a few steps and started to circle around. "I need you to get up slowly. Leave everything. Just stand up and back away."

"It's all around me," I said.

Vincent caught my eye, and I knew whatever this was, it was trouble. "Don't let it touch you."

"What is it?" I asked.

"It's the end," Vincent said. Once the words were out, I felt something break inside him. He moved around to stand in front of me. Then he sat down. He was only a few yards away, but I couldn't reach him. "It's the void. I can't move it, I can't lure it away, and I can't keep it from taking us."

"Then you need to get farther away," I said. "Move back while you can."

He shook his head. "I'm not leaving you."

I rubbed my forehead, trying to get my fevered brain to work. While I looked around, I tried to get a feel for the thing.

"Why is it circling me?" I asked. "I thought it just moved in and swallowed people."

"Maybe it's curious." His voice remained stoic, but his eyes were shining, full of unshed tears. "I know I was when I met you."

I studied the shapeless form, and sensed the atmosphere around us, but waited to reach for the Path.

It wasn't only inquisitive. There was ire as well. Curiosity and anger curled up together and aimed at the world. That couldn't come from an unthinking killing machine.

"I don't know how long we have," Vincent said. "But I need you to know that I love you."

"And I love you," I said, "but I really need a minute to think this through."

"Had we been given the chance, I wanted to spend our lives together. Although I guess we are. It's just shorter than I wanted."

"You can still get away," I said, trying to study the haze, looking for something, anything, that might stand out.

Vincent shook his head. "You go, I go."

"That's the dumbest thing I've ever heard," I said. "And you better believe we're going to talk about that when we get home."

He smiled softly.

The thing started to close in and fear stabbed my heart. I rose to my feet, despite being unsteady. The Path came to me like an old friend.

Looking around, I gasped at the Path the void made.

Vincent was on his feet as well, anger pulsing from him. "This can't happen." He began to prowl around.

The void wasn't an inanimate object destroying everything or an animal, stalking its prey, but the Path was complex and shifting—it was thinking.

And it was pissed.

Vincent seemed to be feeding it even more anger.

"Stop moving," I said quickly. I willed myself not to fall, though my muscles grew more and more tired. I tried to set my fear aside and think of something happy.

Of course, Vincent was at the top of the list. I pulled up the feeling of the love I had for Vincent, and it was overwhelming, surprising even me when I released it.

The emotion hit Vincent hard. He stared at me for a few heartbeats, our eyes locked together. Then he took a step closer.

"No!" I shouted at him. "Stay where you are. Don't move."

The void's Path showed confusion, and I guess I could understand why. Emotion wasn't the best language to use when meeting an entity for the first time.

I licked my lips and squeezed my hands together tight. "I need you to promise me something," I said to Vincent while concentrating on the void.

His eyes pinched together and he looked wary, but said nothing, waiting.

"If this doesn't work, I want you to go back home. Tell our friends and family what happened."

"You can't ask me--"

"I can and I am." I gritted my teeth and closed my eyes. "I love you."

I plunged my hand into the void's Path.

When I opened my eyes again, I saw from *inside* the void. It felt as though we merged together becoming one entity and it showed me why it was shrouded with anger.

We were scared, and approached someone. If it was intelligent, it didn't communicate. It batted its hand at us.

We could sense it. The annoyance and fear. It lasted for a fraction of a second, and then the person was gone. We pulled back, not sure what happened. After that we floated across the strange new landscape. We wandered and listened. We found another person.

The moment we touched them, they were gone.

An empty loneliness crept in. We discovered someone else, but with the same results. Again and again we tried. Desperate to find someone. Anyone.

Then people ran from us. We withdrew and hid away until the isolation became too much.

We watched.

We attempted to communicate.

We gave up.

We wandered aimlessly, not caring where we went or who was in our way. Our people were lost. There was only us.

And then there was her. She sensed us and sought us out. She spoke to us. We didn't understand, but it didn't matter. She shared a piece of herself with us, filling the hollow space inside.

Then she grabbed us. We attempted to run away, not wanting for her to disappear. But she didn't touch us with flesh. Using the feelings she gave us, she ripped us apart.

We screamed and cursed, but something was wrong. We weren't empty, yet we were no longer whole.

THE VOID BACKED AWAY. I gasped and fell to the ground. I wasn't surprised to find tears running down my face. I was startled when Vincent tried to pull me up. Having a body at all startled me. Breathing hurt and felt distinctly unnatural.

Vincent started to drag me away, but stopped. Then he sat down, pulled me to him, and held me.

"The void shifted and I managed to get to you," he said after a while. "But we can't get back out."

There was no way for me to answer. Being in my body was difficult. I was heavy and felt drawn to the ground.

It was Vincent's arms around me that helped me fully come back to myself. When I hugged him back, he let out a deep breath and gripped me tighter.

"I need the bag," I said. My voice was still a whisper, but the sound seemed to carry and echo.

Vincent pulled back enough to look around. He reached out, then hesitated. "There's no way to reach it."

I stared at the hovering mass. I know it didn't understand me, but I kept my eyes on it and nodded to the backpack.

It took a moment, but the void backed away. When the bag was free, I had to urge Vincent again to get the bag.

"I have no idea what you did," Vincent said as he grabbed the bag. "But please, never do it again."

I smiled and shook my head. There was no way I could agree to that, so it was the best I could do.

Vincent dropped the backpack next to me, and then I dumped it out while he settled down behind me, wrapping an around me again. I poked through everything that fell out, then felt around inside the bag's pockets. It took some time, but I found the necklace and pulled it out.

"I'm not sure that's a good idea," Vincent said, though it was without much conviction.

"The void is sentient," I said. "It has thoughts, memories, and emotion. Someone came here and tore out parts of it." I wasn't sure why, but I couldn't bring myself to say that a Reader did this. "It deserves to get those parts of itself back."

"Parts?" Vincent sighed. "We only have one piece."

"We only have one here, but we know where another lives."

"You can't ask me to bring you back here."

I wanted to argue, but I didn't have the strength or voice.

"Later. We can talk later. Right now, I need to finish this." The haze still surrounded us, waiting for me. What would happen if it didn't like what I had to say? "You probably shouldn't be touching me when I do this."

Vincent let out a bark of mirthless laughter. "If you think I'm letting go, you're crazy."

I licked my lips again and eyed the void. I wasn't sure how long it would wait.

"And if you die, but I survive?" I asked. "What happens then?"

"That's *really* not fair," Vincent said.

"I think our odds are better doing it my way."

A frustrated huff of air escaped Vincent. I leaned in and kissed him. Gently at first, then as though it were the last kiss we'd ever have.

And if this didn't work, it would be. When we finally broke apart, I wore a contented smile.

"I hate this," Vincent said. "I don't think it's wise to touch it again."

"You'll be able to yell at me all you want later," I said.

He shook his head, but released me and scooted back. Not far, but I knew it was the best I was going to get.

Before I could talk myself out of it, I put my hand back into the Path of the void.

There was no language between us, only stories shown through our memories. As best as was able, I showed the void what happened to both pieces I had found. This one and the one that hid inside my turtle.

I tried to tell it that I couldn't return the other part right away. My plan had been to hand over the necklace and let the person take it from there. But we both realized quickly that the tiny piece inside the necklace had to be released, and the only one here that could do that was me. There was no way around it.

The first time I encountered a piece of the void, it ended up turning into something much like a black hole. Once it left its containment it began sucking everything into it. If my current attempt to release the void didn't work, I knew there wouldn't be a chance to warn Vincent. We'd be sucked into a whirling vortex of nothingness before either of us figured out things had gone wrong.

If I didn't try to release it, I'm pretty sure our fate would be the same. The void would close in before we would know what was happening.

I wasn't sure if the void understood me or not, but I set to work trying to release the piece that had been stolen away. It took time to find the Path trapped in the necklace.

My mind began to fog over, but I slowly peeled back the Path and set the soul shard free. I was beyond spent and didn't even think about trying to contain the piece when it left the necklace.

Still, no black hole formed. The person surrounding us wavered, or maybe it was me. A melancholy atmosphere rolled off the void as it backed away. I was pretty sure it didn't like me or any other person stuck between the worlds, but I was the only one it could connect with.

The loneliness the void felt hollowed me out. My heart hurt for the person who had been treated so badly and never had anyone to turn to.

I wasn't sure if it was the right thing to do, but the Path of the void seemed safe to touch. Before I lost contact with it, I visualized the clouds of color. I urged the void to try to approach one, but carefully.

Once again, I wasn't sure it understood me, but it didn't seem as angry when it backed further away.

"It's safe now," I said, wiping tears from my face.

Vincent wrapped his arms around me. "Are you okay?"

I shook my head. "It's heartbreaking."

He brushed my cheek softly. "You can fill me in later. Right now, though, you're pale and feverish. We need to get you out of here."

"How far away are we from where we can leave? If I stop reading, I can't be sure I'll be awake."

He hugged me tighter. "Let it go. I've got you."

I knew I was leaving him alone to fend for us, but I had to stop reading. I squeezed his hand and stepped away from my power.

CHAPTER
TEN

I'm not sure when the rhythmic beep entered my consciousness, but it took up residence in my dreams until it became too annoying to ignore. When I opened my eyes, I wasn't surprised to find myself in a hospital bed.

What I wasn't ready for was the extravagant nature of the room. It might as well have been a fancy hotel room where they happened to add medical equipment. The noise of the heart monitor seemed out of place, and it didn't fit with the opulence of the room.

The man in the corner looked as though he belonged in such a rich atmosphere. He was handsome and dressed casually, but in it wasn't the run-of-the-mill jeans and t-shirt. His clothes, from shirt to shoes, screamed money.

He seemed comfortable and at ease in the room, but he was a stranger, and must have been watching me as I slept, so he made me distinctly uncomfortable.

I pulled awkwardly at my blanket and became immediately distracted by the silky feel of the fabric.

"Ms. Heidrich," the man said, standing. "It's good to see you awake. Finally."

I raised an eyebrow, offended, but since I had no idea where I was or who I was with, I didn't want to show the fullness of my indignation. "Nearly dying tends to make me tired. Where am I?"

"Welcome to Saska," the man said. "For the moment, you are in a private medical facility."

The name of the city was familiar. Taylor, Logan, and Vincent had mentioned the place while we were in the mountains.

"And you are?"

"You can call me Scout. Assuming you follow the rules, there's a good chance you won't see me again."

I closed my eyes and shook my head, which I regretted when the vertigo kicked in. "Rules?"

"You are confined to this room until your file has been reviewed. Once you've been released by our medical personnel, you will be given a list of locations you are allowed to go. For an AIR agent, that is usually limited to the airport or nearest car rental facility."

Confined? An unexpected grin appeared on my face.

"Is there a problem?"

"No. I was just thinking about the last time a group of people tried to lock me up."

"AIR agents are not allowed here. If you cause any trouble, you will be asked to leave immediately, with or without medical recommendation."

I rolled my eyes. "Are you my doctor? Because if you are, your bedside manner sucks."

"I run a security firm in the city. You are here at the request of Eva and Vincent Pironus. Considering your condition, their appeal was reluctantly granted."

"Is Vincent okay?" I asked.

"The last he was seen, he was with his sister," Scout said. He pulled out his phone and scrolled through it. "It looks like we're having difficulty pulling your file together. Let your nurse know if there's anything you need—you could be here a while."

"Do I at least get a phone call?"

Scout sighed. "Give me the name of the person you want to contact, and I'll check on it."

"Check on it?"

"AIR has a tenuous relationship with this city. The fact that you're here at all is an anomaly."

"That sounds like me," I muttered, thinking that everything about me ended up irregular. "I'd like to call my grandmother. It's not like she's going to collect information about whatever you do here." I grinned again. "Actually, with me here, that's probably exactly what she's doing. But trust me, there's no way to stop her."

Scout narrowed his eyes at me.

I shrugged. "Don't glare at me like that. She's psychic. There's not much anyone can do about that."

"Her name?" Scout asked.

"Margaret Callaway. I also need to reach my partner to check in."

"You are to have no contact with AIR at this time. Your arrival will be reported to them."

"Are you sure? His name is Logan Seale. AIR agent or not, I know he's been here before."

Scout gave me an indecipherable look.

Although, I guess it doesn't have to be indecipherable. Without closing my eyes, I reached out to the Path. It was easier to move into the flow than I expected. Not as effortless as it had been between worlds, but still more fluid than usual.

When I looked at Scout, my eyes widened. I'd never seen a Path like his before. I watched colors twirl through him as though in a dance. That harmony surrounded a bright central glow, which was muted by a dark enclosure.

He held power—a lot of strength dammed up, wanting to be released.

"Ms. Heidrich," Scout snapped. "I'm not sure you're listening."

Red, scratchy marks interrupted the performance of his Path, but only for a moment. As I watched, parts of his Path reached out to land on his surroundings, leaping from object to object. The probes made his dark brown skin glow. Many tendrils reached in my direction, but I had no idea why.

"I'm sorry," I said, unable to turn away. "I've just never met anyone like you before." I closed my eyes and pushed away the Path.

Exhaustion draped over me like a friend waiting in the wings. The machines started making different noises, which drilled into my head.

"Sorry," I repeated. "What were you saying?"

When I glanced up, Scout wasn't there, but men and women wearing lab coats were hurrying into the room.

I was going to ask where the man went, and ask once again for a phone call, but I fell asleep before the words came out.

Sometime later, an argument in the hall roused me. I was vaguely interested, but still too tired to be invested.

The next time I woke, I was more myself, and as a bonus, I was alone. There were no strange men lurking in the corners of the room. There was an almost obnoxiously large vase of flowers next to the bed, and I sincerely doubted they were from Vincent. Those weren't his style.

Then again, with this type of room, they could have been something that arrived every morning. Examining my quarters more closely I realized I probably should have asked how much this was costing me.

I found a remote and raised myself to a sitting position before clicking the call button. It was past time to figure out what was happening.

A man answered the call. He brought me ice water and talked nonstop from the moment he entered. I couldn't fit in many questions and he wasn't actually giving me any information. The only thing I knew was that he was giddy because Mr. Storm would be in to meet me.

When I asked if that was my doctor, the man laughed and said the doctor would be back in the morning. After that he stopped gushing long enough to order food and showed me how the remote blinds worked, along with the TV and bed features, of which there were many.

When I was alone, I opened the blinds and from my bed I stared out into a dark and stormy night. It was an odd view with bright lights of towering skyscrapers and sprawling city which seemed to climb in the distance before

disappearing into darkness as though abruptly cut off. Pretty, but I was more interested to see what it looked like during the day.

I needed perspective in more ways than one.

Why hadn't I asked what time it was? I had no idea how long I slept. It seemed like ages had passed, but it was always hard to tell when I overextended myself. Sometimes I woke up the next morning, and other times it was days later.

For some reason, I thought it was the latter, because I felt heavy and detached. That kind of loneliness took time to build.

Unless of course, it was a memory left behind after meeting the void. That poor person. Lost from its own world and living in one where it could touch nothing.

Someone knocked at the door and I called for them to come

in, despite the door starting to open before my words had come out. More than anything, I wanted it to be Vincent, sadly it was another unfamiliar man.

Admittedly, he was a handsome stranger, wearing a suit which appeared to be tailored perfectly for him.

But he wasn't Vincent.

"Ms. Heidrich," the man said, coming over. "I'm Jackson Storm. It's a pleasure to meet you."

He offered his hand which I shook and waited for further information.

"How are you feeling?"

"Cranky," I lied. There was no way I would tell a stranger how I really felt at the moment.

"Well, let's see if we can fix that. Your doctor said you're well enough for visitors, so you'll be getting out of this place before long."

My eyes narrowed. "And straight to the airport, I suppose."

He laughed, but it sounded unnatural. "Never mind that. You're welcome to come and go. The city is open to you."

I frowned and wondered what had caused the shift in attitude. "Mr. Storm--"

"Please, call me Jack. You know, Logan had wonderful things to say about you."

My frown left. Of *course* Logan could turn things around. "That's good to hear."

"In fact, he's on his way, along with your mother and grandmother. They'll be staying at a lovely hotel, right across the street. As soon as you're discharged, you'll have a room there as well, for as long as you'd like. I want you all to consider yourselves guests of Storm Enterprises."

"I'm sorry, Mr. Storm—" I saw him smile and open his mouth, so rushed to correct myself. "I mean Jack. I'm not sure what's going on here. I have no idea who you are, or why the change of heart. I'm still an AIR agent. I thought being here was against the rules."

"Those rules weren't made for someone like you." Jack smiled broadly. "No, Logan and Mr. Pironus, along with a very few select other agents, are allowed to come and go as they like. I want you and your family to have the same access."

He wanted something. There had to be a reason for all this.

"And my best friend--our other partner, Rider? He'd be allowed to come here as well?" I pressed.

Jack's smile dropped momentarily, but it returned quickly. "Of course. I want you to be comfortable."

"Why?" The question was blunt, but he clearly had an agenda.

"Straight to the point. I like it. I'm going to be candid with you. I want to offer you a job."

"Me? To do what? Why?"

"Power like yours comes around once in a lifetime, if we're lucky. Getting information about you was difficult, but I'm very impressed with what I've heard."

I stared at him for a moment, as though considering what he said. Instead, I took the time to step into my power. I was immediately greeted with a Path similar to Scout's.

"What kind of job?" I asked. It was almost impossible to stop myself from openly staring at the man. The same fluidity I had seen in Scout filled Jack along with eruptions of power breaking through. Even when forced to change from inter-fering burst of energy, the patterns of power merged beau-tifully.

The main difference was Jack's strength. This man *dwarfed* everyone I'd ever seen. His power was locked away like Scout's, but the thought of being around when that lock opened terri-fied me.

"Research, mostly. But if that doesn't interest you, I know

Scout could use you in security. In this city there are hundreds of opportunities to put your skills to good use."

"You haven't even seen what I can do."

"That is a very good point. I planned to wait before running a little test, but I have to admit my curiosity is piqued and waiting isn't in my skill-set."

A spike of anticipation bolted through him like lightning. He pulled a gun, pointed it at me, and fired.

The air in front of me turned solid quickly, which was practically an automatic response. A part of me knew Jack moved slower than he'd needed to, and that his aim was a few feet too wide, but those thoughts were overruled with a gun in the mix.

The bullet hung in midair. I grabbed Jack's Path and yanked it back, slamming him into a wall. Less than a second later, Scout ran into the room, gun aimed at me.

I really hated it when people pointed weapons at me.

"Hold!" Jack shouted from his position on the floor where he landed. The hint of laughter behind the words seriously pissed me off. "It was a rubber bullet."

Scout didn't lower his gun, and I definitely didn't appreciate his finger on the trigger. The bullet would never reach me if he fired, but that wasn't the point.

Jack started to get to his feet, and this time he did laugh.

Another man sauntered into the room and leaned against a wall. He appeared to be mildly amused as well, but his attention was directed at Jack

"I do apologize," Jack said. "I promise you I meant no harm. It was only a test."

I glared at him. "I'm barely awake and still in the hospital and you shot at me? That was your test?"

"Which you passed beautifully, young lady," Jack said.

Anger filled me so intensely I became frozen in indecision about what to do first.

It was always best to start with weapons.

I grinned cruelly at Jack. At the same time, I grabbed the Path of both guns, Jack's and Scout's, and yanked them away from their owners.

Scout had another out by the time the first clattered to the floor, and according to his Path, he meant business. I leaned forward in the bed and wrapped his second weapon in my power.

It pushed my limits, and I knew it.

It wasn't a smart thing to do, but it wasn't going to stop me.

Much like I'd compacted the air to shield myself, I took the Path of Scout's gun and compressed it. There was a lot of resistance, but within moments, the barrel smashed itself together.

Jack still grinned broadly. Disarming them did very little to demonstrate my outrage. I needed something more dramatic.

Much like the display I had given the gremlins when they locked me up. I eyed the windows and wondered how cold it was outside.

The newcomer stepped forward. He had a wicked half grin on his face as he winked at me.

I gave him a nasty look when he cleared his throat.

"I'm supposed to deliver a message, and this appears to be the most fitting time."

We all turned to him, expectantly.

He looked at ease being the center of attention. "Anala said 'no windows.'"

I glared at him for several seconds, but Mom's name might as well have been a cold bucket of water dumped on me. It amazed me that she had seen something like this from so far away.

Still, I wasn't happy with the message or the situation.

I breathed out heavily and crossed my arms. "Fine. But if another gun gets pointed at me, all bets are off."

"Who's Anala?" Jack asked.

"I have no idea," Chance said. "I don't know what the message means, or how she got my number, but she called and I was intrigued."

Now that the excitement seemed to be over, Jack moved forward and inspected Scout's gun. Scout handed it over, and Jack ran his hands over the crushed metal.

"Outstanding," Jack murmured.

I rolled my eyes and shook my head. At the same time, I dropped my hold on the Paths, but I didn't stop reading. Not because I was worried about another attack, but because of the stranger. He leaned against the wall again, looking amused.

I could have stared at him all day. His Path moved internally like that of the other two, but there was a twist to the flow. The dance inside him was far more complex. I also found it interesting that the power hidden in his core wasn't as well shielded. Fire leaked from its containment.

"Think about my offer," Jack said, still staring at the gun. "I'll have someone call with the details. Scout, I'd like a word, and Chance, I want you in the office first thing tomorrow."

"Ten-thirty it is," Chance said.

Jack shot him a small glare, which quickly disappeared.

Scout went to the corner where I had tossed the weapons. He raised an eyebrow at me.

I shrugged and turned away. He gathered them and started to leave.

"Jack, wait," I called. "I'm curious about something. Why are you so interested in my power when you three have so much of your own?"

Jack's stare was calculating and lasted longer than I was

comfortable with. Then, he left without another word. Scout nodded at me and followed Jack out of the room.

The other man stayed. I leaned back and finally stepped away from my power. My head throbbed and my stomach began to cramp up.

"You called him Jack," the man said. He still wore a mischievous grin that was almost as addictive as Logan's smile.

Even without reading I wanted to stare. I had to force my gaze away and remind myself that I still needed to find Vincent.

I shrugged my shoulders, trying to loosen the tension in my muscles, and scooted to the edge of the bed. "That's what he said to call him. Who are you?"

"Chance. I'm sorry, I knew your room number, but didn't catch your name."

"It's Cassie. Thank you for delivering the message. I don't suppose she mentioned where I could find my clothes, did she?" I remembered where I had been and what happened to my clothes. "Scratch that. Maybe just clothes in general."

"In a hurry to leave?"

It was the stupidest question ever. "Someone just shot at me and guns were pointed at me. I'm not going to sit around and wait for them to decide they want to try again."

Chance dropped into a chair and leaned back, apparently making himself at home. "You don't have to worry about Scout."

"Honestly, I was more concerned about Jack."

"Jack? He rarely leaves the office. Just so you know, you can name your price if you decide to work for him."

"How do you know that?"

"Very few people are asked to call him Jack."

"I don't think I should stick around to see what he has in mind next."

"He said what he wants," Chance said. "He's not going to waste any more time."

I sat on the edge of the bed, unconvinced. "How can you be so sure?"

"He's my brother."

My shoulders slumped. "That doesn't exactly ease my concerns."

"Trust me. He's smart enough to know he pissed you off, and he also understands that to have any prospect of hiring you, he needs to leave you alone."

I relaxed a little. "That makes sense I guess."

"Besides, tomorrow I'm giving him a new project he can obsess over. And, no offense, but you don't look ready to go anywhere," Chance said. "Don't get me wrong, you're cute as hell, but I don't think you should be far from a doctor."

I smiled. "You're probably right. I'm also pretty sure I don't have any clothes, which makes leaving difficult." I eased back in the bed.

Chance eyed me up and down. "When you get out of here, would you like to get together for drinks?" He grinned. "Clothing optional."

Damn he was cute. Cocky, but cute. "Thanks, but I have a boyfriend." I frowned. "I haven't seen him here, but I'm sure he's still around."

"Who's the lucky guy?" Chance asked.

"Vincent Pironis. His sister lives here." I couldn't help but smile when I said his name.

"Pironis has a girl," Chance's smile became more normal with the flirtation removed. "Good for him."

"You know him?"

"Sure. We've hung out a few times. He's a good person."

My grin widened, despite my exhaustion. "He is. That's not the response I normally hear, though."

"You mean because of the Walker thing?"

I nodded.

Chance shrugged. "Let's just say Walkers aren't the only ones to have a bad reputation in this town." His mood shifted and he leaned forward, looking more intent. "You're not having any problems with him as a Walker are you?"

"He frustrates the hell out of me sometimes, but I'm fairly certain the feeling is mutual."

Chance laughed and stood up. "I'm glad to hear it." He pulled a card from his wallet and gave it to me. "Have him call me sometime. We can all go out for drinks."

"Sure," I said. "I'd like that." Having just met Chance, it came as a surprise that I meant what I said.

"Before I go, I have to ask... what would you have done to the windows?"

I grinned. "One time when I was really aggravated and wanted to prove a point, the building I was in ended up needing both a new door and new windows."

"Pironis is a lucky man."

"He is," Vincent said from the door.

My eyes brightened and my insides squeezed together. I wanted to say something, but the words caught in my throat. He was alive.

"Vincent, it's good to see you." Chance's impish grin made another appearance. He held his hand out to Vincent.

Vincent only nodded, and although he came into the room, he avoided moving any closer to Chance. "I didn't expect to see you here."

Chance dropped his hand, but not his smile. "Someone named Anala reached me. I wasn't sure why until I got here. My brother... made a poor first impression."

Vincent's eyes narrowed and he was close enough for me to see they were solid black. "He usually does."

"Speaking of which," Chance said, turning to me. He didn't appear the least bit concerned about Vincent. "If you decide to take the job, don't accept anything less than four hundred thousand."

"That sounds high," I said. *Insane is more like it.*

"Trust me. He'll pay."

"I need a few minutes alone with Cassie," Vincent said. "And I don't have much time."

"Understood," Chance said, moving to leave. "Give me a call before you leave town. It was nice meeting you, Cassie."

He hesitated and looked back to Vincent, but then glanced out the door again and flirtation entered his voice. "Eva, what an unexpected surprise."

Vincent closed his eyes for a moment as Chance left, then shook his head and closed the gap between us.

"I can't tell you how relieved I am to see you're okay," I said.

His eyes cleared, but his smile was tight lipped. Still, he sat down on the bed next to me and took my hand.

"How do you feel?" he asked.

"I'm...recovering." There was no way I could tell him I felt like hell. "I was surprised to have visitors."

"We can talk about that later. By phone."

By phone? My heart fell a little. He always said he couldn't be around people after returning from between the worlds. "You're not staying." A part of me had been worried this would happen.

"I can't."

This close to Vincent I felt his torment. Despite the overuse of my gifts, I stepped into it again.

Vincent was a powder keg ready to blow. He kept a dense

corruption lashed down inside him, yet it was a tenuous hold at best.

"But I had to see you in person," Vincent finished.

I swallowed hard, but nodded. "I think I understand." My eyes teared up. I knew it wouldn't help the situation, though I couldn't seem to stop.

"Please don't," Vincent said. Closing his eyes, he took a few deep breaths.

"It's okay. I really do understand. Sort of, anyway. It doesn't mean I like it." He didn't say anything, so I tried a change in subject. "I see the doctor tomorrow morning."

"I've been getting updates," he said.

"I'm glad you have. I'm not even sure how long I've been here."

His eyebrows knitted together, and I saw the darkness inside him strain against the bonds he created. "They haven't told you anything?"

"I keep waking up at the wrong times, I think." I smiled at him and patted his hand. "The orderly probably would have told me something, but--" I didn't think mentioning Jack right now would be the best idea, so I quickly changed tactics. "I don't know these people. I'm not sure what's safe to say and what's not."

He relaxed some. "This floor and two others are for the Lost and people like you."

I almost corrected him and said 'us,' but I was too worried about him. Pain was etched into his Path, and it wasn't the physical kind.

"Mom, Gran and Logan are on their way," I said at least hoping to help him worry less about me. It seemed to work. "And now that Rider is allowed here, I'm sure he'll come as well. At least if I'm here that long."

"Rider?" His lips turned up a fraction and the maelstrom inside him settled down about the same amount.

Seeing we were headed in the right direction, I reduced my power to the tiniest of streams, knowing that when I let go completely there was no way I'd stay awake.

"You'll have to tell me how that happened. Later," he finished.

"I'm going to be okay," I said. "I feel so much better already."

"I know."

I grinned. "But you had to see me for yourself."

"I did. We also need to talk."

I raised an eyebrow. "That's never a good sign."

He seemed to ignore me. "We had problems between us while traveling between worlds. It's something we need to fix."

"Now?"

His lips twitched up momentarily once again. "Not now. I've never been good at this, but I've never had a reason to be in the past."

My heart squeezed tight.

Vincent shook his head. "I'm messing this up already. What you're feeling right now--that fear and panic--we've both felt it, and it's an issue we can't hide from."

"What are you suggesting?" I asked, trying not to pull back.

He rubbed my hand. "You, Eva, and Rider--you're everything to me. I want you and I to take time to consider what we want and need from each other."

Those words were promising, but I still held reservations. "Time?"

"Communicating hasn't come easy for us, and this is important. When I get home and we're both settled in, we should discuss the possibilities of our future together."

My tension began to unravel. "That doesn't sound so bad."

He smiled. A real, smile open for the world to see. "I hope not, but we really need to think about this, good and bad."

Seeing the smile eased my concerns, though it raised others. Talking about our future together would take me far from my comfort zone. "You're right. This is important and we shouldn't rush it, but we can't cut each other off all that time."

"We won't."

Someone knocked on the door, even though it was still open. Framed in the doorway was a dark-haired woman who could only be Vincent's sister. The resemblance was undeniable. The smile she gave her brother seemed to include me.

At least I hoped it did.

"You wanted me to interrupt you," Eva said.

Vincent nodded, but didn't turn away from me. "I have to go."

Eva gave him a critical look and studied him. "Are you sure you need to?" Eva asked.

I'm not sure what she saw in Vincent, but when I opened my power to read his Path again it was clear he had more control than before.

"I'm certain." He leaned forward and kissed me. The kiss was short, but enough to make me forget about reading or his sister. Too soon he broke apart and strode to the doorway, which was empty. "Eva will come by again so you two can officially meet and I'll call tomorrow afternoon."

"I'm holding you to that," I said.

When he reached the door, he turned back. "I'm not sure what Jackson Storm wanted, but be careful around him."

I grinned. "Don't worry. He's nursing a few bruises, and Chance doesn't think he'll stop by again."

Vincent smiled again, but left the room without saying anything else.

As usual, frustrating as hell... but sweet, too.

COMPLETE WORKS

Complete works by Amanda Booloodian:

AIR Series (In Reading Order)
Stonecoat: Novella 0 (AIR Series Book 0)
Shattered Soul (AIR Series Book 1)
Redcap (AIR Series Book 2)
Broken Paths (AIR Series Book 3)
Stolen Sight (AIR Series Book 4)
Fenrisúlfr: Novella 3.5 (AIR Series 5)
Fractured Worlds (AIR Series Book 6)
Reliquary (AIR Series Book 7)
Never-Ending Nightmare (AIR Series Book 8)
Krampus (AIR Series Book 9)
Eclipsed Pathways (AIR Series Book 10)
Void (AIR Series Book 11)
Marked Soul (AIR Series Book 12)

AIR Series Box Set
AIR Series Books 0-4: Welcome to the Farm
AIR Series Books 5-8: Conspiracy Theory
AIR Series Books 9-12: Redacted

Spellbound Murder Series
Oath Bound (Spellbound Murder Series Book 1)
Grim Magic (Spellbound Murder Series Book 2)
Fallen Witch (Spellbound Murder Book 3)

Spellbound Murder Box Set
Spellbound Murder Complete Trilogy

AIR Series Audiobooks
Stonecoat: Novella 0.5 (AIR Series Book 0)
Shattered Soul (AIR Series Book 1)
Redcap (AIR Series Book 2)
Broken Paths (AIR Series Book 3)
Stolen Sight (AIR Series Book 4)
Fenrisúlfr: Novella 3.5 (AIR Series 5)
Fractured Worlds (AIR Series Book 6)
Reliquary (AIR Series Book 7)
Never-Ending Nightmare (AIR Series Book 8)
Krampus (AIR Series Book 9)
Eclipsed Pathways (AIR Series Book 10)
Void (AIR Series Book 11)
Marked Soul (AIR Series Book 12)

Spellbound Murder Series Audiobooks
Oath Bound (Spellbound Murder Series Book 1)
Grim Magic (Spellbound Murder Series Book 2)
Fallen Witch (Spellbound Murder Book 3)

ABOUT THE AUTHOR

Amanda Booloodian lives in Missouri with her loving, and often times peculiar, husband. She has been passionate about the written word throughout her life. Now, much of her spare time is spent at the computer, delving into worlds accessible only through vivid imagination. In warm weather, when she isn't pounding on the keyboard, she can often be found wandering through the wilderness. Occasionally she gets it into her head to SCUBA dive or to sit back at home and make wine, which can have interesting results and inspire her writing.

You can find out more about Amanda and her writing, including upcoming releases, on www.Booloodian.com. You can also find her on Facebook: Amanda Booloodian - Author and Instagram: AJBooloodian.